What Ifs

Paddy Bostock

A Wings ePress, Inc.
Political Fantasy Novel

Wings ePress, Inc.

Edited by: Jeanne Smith
Copy Edited by: Christie Kraemer
Executive Editor: Jeanne Smith
Cover Artist: Trisha FitzGerald-Jung

All rights reserved

Wings ePress Books
www.wingsepress.com

Copyright © 2019 by: Paddy Bostock
ISBN-13: 978-1-61309-609-3
ISBN-10: 1-61309-609-7

Published In the United States Of America

Wings ePress Inc.
3000 N. Rock Road
Newton, KS 67114

What They Are Saying About
What Ifs

"First off, I'd like to start with how the book has captured my attention from the start. It introduced our main character in a poetic way. Very deep and almost sensual.

He was, in his own opinion, odd. Very interested in only himself but in a non-self-absorbed way. He never realizes his true potential, until he meets Gabi, who makes him realize all the good he has done.

It's a romantic take on how a person struggles to perceive one's inner self despite the many obstacles one faces. People around you notice you and are willing to help, if you'd only let them. Some creatures we do not see may offer aid as well. And like many others, we must use our hearts to see them.

This book transcends all the good things life has to offer and how you must discover yourself to find these good things. They come often. Only we do not know they are there.

A great read about adventure, life, philosophy, and a bit of fantasy; this book is truly a treasure for someone who's trying to find the meaning of life or just having a good cup of coffee in a rose garden."

—Isabella Rose Meillure

https://dawninreverie.blogspot.com/2019/06/what-ifs-by-paddy-bostock-review.html

:

"Fair Warning: If you're looking for a light-hearted and fluffy read, this is not it!

This is not my first book by this author and it won't be my last. I love the unique and rich writing style of Paddy that is quite rare these days. With so many books coming out every other day, one would think they have so many choices, but most of them are fluffy reads. On the other hand, Paddy's books are intriguing and enticing.

What Ifs is one such book ... which keeps you riveted to the tale from the beginning to the end. I planned to read it in one sitting but ended up pushing half of it for today. It's a story about the two MCs, James and Gabi, with other characters adding to the story. I particularly loved the Elf part (Kay Cee)—funny and interesting.

Throughout the book you're often left wondering if it's one of the scenarios, or happening in real life, but the book keeps you engaged. I also liked James' brother William and his antics. Just like the title states, it's a lot of what-if scenarios, and is an interesting read.

If you're looking for a mysterious and thrilling ride, you have it with *What Ifs*."

—Sherin Lloyd
https//www.goodreads.com/review/show/2884382494

"The title of the book caught my attention and intrigued me right away. It brought me back to my philosophical roots. I had spent most of my life pursuing the "what-ifs" of life. And now I had the honour of reading a story with the same theme.

The story starts in a pensive setting where peace and order exist even if for a brief moment because it is a pristine natural escape away from the maddening crowd and all the chaos that modern life throws at all of us—a place for a thinker to go and rest.

James Cockburn is a thinker and an artist. He lives in the world of his imagination. And nothing seems more pleasing to him than imagining what would happen if this or that arose. He loves to reflect on the human being in an existential way.

Being an existentialist, he was naturally pessimistic. His life was anything but happy. His wife left him and his upbringing and early years were hard, with boarding schools and nannies. He felt alone and probably isolated.

He taught at Heidelberg University and was a writer with quite a following. One of the people who admired him looked him up and ultimately found him through the internet. Her name was Gabriele. From his writing, she believed they were kindred spirits.

From the first time they met in his peaceful place, there was something about her that intrigued him. He didn't believe in love at first sight, but could this really be happening? He'd had a bunch of unfulfilling relationships with women, so he never believed true love would find him. He also never thought he was physically attractive enough for real love. But when he met Gabi, something was stirring within him that he had never felt and it was scaring him. Was it really true love? Lust? Infatuation?

As the days turned into weeks and months, things got quite complicated. His artist brother William was murdered in quite a horrific way. His partner, Stephanie, seemed to think James had something to do with the murder, while Gabi got pregnant and wedding bells rang out for the two of them.

Yet all the while, he was still a writer and thinker, asking himself *what if* questions. He never liked crime novels, but now he had a real life murder investigation opening up for his brother, William.

Do Gabi and James live happily ever after? Can James hang onto the immediate love he felt for Gabi when they first met? Who really murdered William? Those questions I will leave up to the reader to investigate.

This story is wonderfully written and portrayed. Paddy Bostock is at his best, weaving inquiry with philosophical questions as well as open and raw love in this unforgettable murder mystery. I love the story and will be recommending it to my friends."

Rating: 5 stars
—Irene S. Roth
irenesroth.wordpress.com

Dedication

To Dani, with love.

* * *

One

"So long as man has air to breathe, and eyes can see. So long as this lives, it will bring life to thee." Such was the inscription on the little brass plaque on the backrest of the bench between two beds of roses called Diamond Jubilee and Blue For You, and opposite two ancient giant swamp cypresses in Queen Mary's Gardens in Regent's Park.

It was James Cockburn's favourite place on the planet; the haven he always sought when needing to escape life's daily horrors: personal, political, ecological... Where with little effort, normally for an hour or so, he could share with Nature its silent wisdoms and make believe there was still some order in the world. What the "this" in the plaque's message referred to—the bench itself or the wider ambience of what he thought of as The Rose Gardens' special magic—he had never decided. But it was a poem, after all, and poems were metaphorical, weren't they, so it could mean either or both. All he knew was whoever had engraved the inscription must have been a person after his own troubled mind. Long dead no doubt, but living on in those words.

So that's where James was sitting on this late June evening. Chewing on an apple while watching two black swans—clarinet swans, he thought—gliding up and down the lake and a gaggle of moorhen chicks stalking about on their outsized feet pecking at things, while their mother hovered around behind them. Overhead, seagulls and pigeons waited for any passerby with food, then swooped down to compete with the magpies and squirrels also ready to pounce on titbits. The place was peculiarly bucolic, given it was little more than a stone's throw from the bedlam of gridlocked central London, and James was glad to see folk from many different countries sharing with him its joys. Yes, there was the usual twenty-first century contingent of morons so fixated by their smartphones they had no idea *where* they were. And yes, tourists in their thousands preferred the tacky baubles of nearby Camden Market to anything non-manmade, but to offset them, there were still those who found their way beyond the children's crusade and, evidently, gloried in what they found. Sniffed the splendid display of roses, then took close-up photos of them, stared at the swamp cypresses' breathing tube "knees" and wondered what they were, and clucked along with the moorhen chicks. Orientals, Asians, Europeans, Brits...James liked that. A relief indeed it was to see there were at least some people left in the world with an eye for beauty that didn't come out of a tin. A shame so many of them, even the once svelte French, must have spent their childhoods and adolescences eating burgers and fries, but such was life in these troubled times. Maybe, they ate to stay sane. Maybe, they would do *any*thing, momentarily, to forget a world that contained the pernicious presidents of the USA and Russia, not to speak of the asininity of homegrown Brexiteers. But that was the human being for you; the blind despoiler of the very planet that provided sustenance for all species of animal.

To ban these ever present reflections from his mind, James switched his attention back to the scent of roses, the luxuriance of the swamp cypresses, the blithe indifference of the non-human creatures, the late afternoon light flickering across the lake's waters—how had Monet ever managed to paint *that*—chewed at his apple and debated whether to roll himself a cigarette, and let the nicotine divert his attention from human frailty, and revivify his dream of a better world. Maybe one day, he'd put the dream in one of his stories. He was a writer, after all—at least in the sense that he wrote—and who *else*'s responsibility was it to posit alternatives to the status quo?

It was as he was struggling with the cigarette and authorial decisions that he became aware beside his bench of a non-rose-type perfume, more likely Chanel some number or another, and what he took to be another human presence. And, turning his head to check this out, there sniffing at one of the fragrant yellow Diamond Jubilees stood a tall, slender, blonde with the best bottom James had seen in St Mary's Gardens since he couldn't remember when. "Sculpted" went nowhere near to describing its perfection. She smiled at him as he turned.

"Nice. A Golden Celebration, I think," she said in English, impeccable apart from the trace of a German accent.

"Jubilee. *Diamond* Jubilee," said James, returning to his apple and chomping it down almost to the core.

"*Ach so.* May I sit with you?" she said.

"Um," said James, glancing to his left and right where there were empty benches on either side. It wasn't as though he had movie star looks or anything. He was no Gollum, but no Brad Pitt either. But Fräulein Super Bum was apparently oblivious to his hesitancy. Before he could say boo to a moorhen, she'd sat herself down beside him and was looking at him as if he were interesting.

~ * ~

"Gabriele," she said thrusting out a hand. "But my friends call me Gabi."

"Hi, Gabriele, just a minute," James said, transferring the apple core to his left hand and wiping the right one on his jeans ready for shaking. That's what Germans did when they met each other. Shook hands. He knew that from the time he'd lived in their country.

Gabriele/Gabi waited patiently while he performed the palm cleansing with one hand and tossed the apple core at a magpie with the other. A *single* magpie, more was the pity. One for misery, two for joy... James could be superstitious. Nonetheless, once he'd ritualistically muttered, "Hello, Mister Magpie, and how's your fine wife today? Very well, I hope," he allowed the fräulein to greet him formally. The grip was firm, more of a man-type grip, and she held on for the better part of a minute while gazing into his eyes, causing him to avert them, and take an unnatural interest in the magpie's success or otherwise at apple-core eating. For the record, it was doing pretty well. Standing on the fruit with one foot while tearing at it with its beak.

"And *your* name?" she said.

"James."

She nodded. "Nice name."

"It's all right," he said while she tossed back her hair and finger-combed it down over her shoulders. Most blokes would have ogled lasciviously and, thinking this was their lucky day, gone for the kill. But James wasn't most blokes. All he did was to edge sideways along the bench and offer the grimace he thought of as a smile.

"You could call me Gabi if you wanted."

"Okay." James checked his watch as if in expectation of an urgent appointment.

"You have to go? So soon?"

"No, no, it's just—"

"You are a busy man."

"Sort of," James lied, having no plans at all for the rest of the day apart from struggling through the final edit of his latest novel. Its title was *World's End*, and it had a complexly parallel narrative interweaving the collapse of Western democracy since the arrival of the madmen in The White House and The Kremlin with the failure of its hero's unhappy connection to a woman called Esmeralda.

"May I ask what you do?"

Hiatus while James thought about this.

Gabi looked concerned. "Are you feeling quite all right? You are looking pale," she said, leaning in towards him.

"Fine, fine. Never better," he chirped Britishly. You know how it is with Brits. How they can be dragged bleeding and crippled from under a pantechnicon and still assure the ambulance guys they're fine thanks.

"Good, good. Of this, I am glad to hear."

Gabi stared off, and James hoped she was losing interest in him. But no. Once the staring off was over, she fixed him with her azure eyes again, and said, "You are an artist, I think. A man of sensitivity."

James chuckled. He couldn't help it. The reason his ex had given for leaving him was he had as much sensitivity as the Morrow character in *The Catcher in the Rye*, i.e. about as much as a toilet seat. James's ex taught American lit at King's College London. Her idea of conversation was quoting famous American authors. Frankly, James was pretty glad when she became his ex. Love, in James's view, could not flourish on quotes alone.

"This is funny?" said Gabi, smiling broadly to display a mouthful of large and perfect pearly teeth.

James shook his head. Not in negation, merely in recognition of life's little ironies. It was during this headshake that strange shifts began happening in his head, shifts he was later to attribute to Heisenberg's Uncertainty Principle, which he interpreted as meaning weird things could happen out of the blue without anybody knowing where they came from or where they were going.

Anyway, so it was then he said, "Look, how would you fancy a cup of coffee? There's a café to our left just past the Japanese garden. It'll only take a few minutes to get there."

"*Mit der größten Freude*," she said. (With the greatest pleasure— or joy, if you want to get picky about it.) "*Vielen Dank*," she added.

"*Bitte schön*," James replied.

"So...you speak German." She laughed before taking his hand, and they began making their way under the weeping willows, past the gilt-encrusted entrance gates, past a whole lot more roses and towards the café.

"*Ein bißchen*" (a bit), said James.

Gabi nodded. Knowingly.

~ * ~

The coffee was excellent. They also had a slice each of *Schwarzwälder Kirschtorte* to make Gabi feel more at home. What with the sunshine, the coffee, and the cake, James was starting to feel almost at ease, a state of being with which he had little familiarity.

"So, Gabriele..." he said as the pair sat at a table beneath a sunshade on the café's forecourt as the dying sun went down.

"*Gabi*."

"Gabi. Where do you come from in Germany?"

"Heidelberg." She smiled through a mouthful of *Kirschtorte*. "At least these days. Originally, I am from Berlin."

"Both beautiful cities in their different ways."

"You have been to them?"

"Some years ago now."

"As a tourist or...?"

"Berlin, yes. In Heidelberg, I taught English at the university. Walked the philosophers' path most days."

"Ah, *der Philosophenweg*. Many times too I walk this path. Wonderful view down over the Neckar."

"And what do you do there?"

Gabi laughed. "Teach English at the university. We have something in common you and I, James."

As she said this, a single magpie hopped towards their table evidently attracted by the cherry cake. That made another single magpie in the space of forty-four minutes. James had this Tourettes-type thing with time. He liked to check it regularly. He was also worried about the magpie. Did a person have to see two magpies *together* for joy to happen, or could two single ones in different places count? And if so, within what time frame? Not a whole day obviously, so two minutes, three minutes, what? *Forty-four* minutes seemed a bit of a stretch. And anyway, what if this were the *same* magpie who'd flown over from where he last saw it eating his apple core? No way could *that* be counted as two and, therefore, elicit joy. Diluted misery maybe, but definitely not joy.

Gabi noticed his distraction.

"There is something the matter, James?" she said. "You are looking pale again."

"No, no, I'm fine. Just...you know," he said, much of the unaccustomed ease draining away to be replaced by the unnamable fear which had accompanied him ever since the button came off his school jacket when he was six years old, and he had to run all the way home to have it sewn back on again by Nanny. That nagging sense there was something out of place that needed fixing, which these days extended to almost every aspect of his life. Call it existential angst. Call it neurosis. Call it anything you want.

"You're *sure*?" Gabi frowned. Gabi the perfect human female specimen, the kind Hitler would have made into a poster girl for Aryans.

"Look, perhaps I should be going," James said, checking his watch again and rising from his seat. "It's all been very pleasant, but…"

Gabi wasn't having any of that, though. "No, no. Please, sit down again," she said in a tone that brooked no dissent. "And I will help you, Mister Sensitive Artist."

James ran his hand through the mousy hair he'd allowed to grow long so it fell over his ears in a way that hadn't been fashionable for decades. Nowadays, men had short back and sides with cleverly crafted top bits and sported stubble at the very least. Many had big bushy beards to prove they were proper men. James had tried these new looks in a variety of forms, but none had worked. The proxy beard caused him to look like a bum-fluff schoolboy, and the full version would only grow in isolated tufts that wouldn't join up together, so he'd shaved both versions off again. Also there were tiny hints of grey and white in there, which he didn't like at all. And *this* was the bloke the blonde *Übermensch* was promising to help.

To what end, he wondered. Nonetheless, he sat back down as commanded. That was another of James's weaknesses: acquiescence. "No More Mister Nice Guy," he would tell myself while shaving every morning. But had it ever worked? The hell it had, so he'd been left to suffer from what he termed The Tyranny of Niceness.

~ * ~

"James, I have a suggestion," said Gabi, sixteen minutes later by James's watch as he squirmed on his seat staring at his slice of only half-eaten *Schwarzwälder Kirschtorte*. "Are you listening?"

"Mmm."

"You are sure?" Said like a schoolteacher to an inattentive child.

"I'm listening. Suggestion, you said."

"*Genau*."(exactly).

"So say it," said Mister Nicer-Than-He-Wanted-To-Be-Guy, skimming off a cherry with his fork while peering at the magpie, which was also peering at him. Not very joyously, he reckoned.

"Why don't you come home with me?"

"*Home* with you?"

"To my place. It is not far away, and I have the black cab app."

"App?"

James had heard the word before but wasn't entirely sure what it meant. Yet one more item from the peculiar lexicon of computer parlance he feared would one day leave him stranded in a terrifying time warp unable to fend for himself. Not unlike the possibly apocryphal story of his maternal grandmother who, on the introduction of decimal coinage in 1971 when she was aged ninety-one, had simply held out handfuls of the new cash to shopkeepers, and said, "Help yourself." Now, it was her grandson's turn. The last time James had tried to pay for his groceries with currency rather than plastic, he had been stared at by the checkout girl as if he were a visitor from the planet Zog.

"This," said Gabi, taking a smartphone from her shoulder bag, tapping at it, then holding it up before his eyes to reveal a screen full of bizarre and, to James, meaningless icons. "Life at the touch of a button."

Which was the very reason he loathed smartphones and refused to buy one. His life lived at the touch of someone else's button? No chance. What if he had his identity stolen by Facebook or Cambridge Analytica? James had quite enough identity problems without it being hijacked altogether, thank you very much.

"Oh," he said, none the wiser.

Gabi sighed, but more in sympathy than criticism. "Silly boy," she said, taking his hand and stroking it, which James found more soothing than he might have expected. Not normally one of those touchy, touchy, feely, feely types wasn't James Cockburn, the very opposite, in fact. He still embarrassed even himself when he involuntarily flinched at someone's well-intentioned pat on the back, for example. Poor parenting, he always assumed. Or in his case poor *nanny*ing, seeing as Mater and Pater were always too preoccupied enriching themselves to bother about him or his brother William.

"We can be there in fifteen minutes, if the traffic is good," Gabi continued, rising from her chair and heading off to pay the bill. With her smartypants phone, no doubt.

"I don't know. I mean...um," James said at her retreating top-of-the-range bottom.

The magpie hopped onto the table and took to pecking at the remains of the cherry cake without so much as a by-your-leave. James could have sworn the bird winked at him. He shook his head, delved into his jacket pocket, found the phial of Valium he had acquired below the counter from a rogue pharmacist in Soho, shook thirty drops into the remains of his coffee and swallowed hard. If he were to be spirited away by an app, it would be only semi-conscious.

"Ready? The cab's on its way," said Gabi on her return.

Two

James remembered nothing of the cab ride apart from woozy dreams. It was only when Gabi took his febrile hand and led him to the portals of a Victorian-looking building across the road from the railway station, that his eyes snapped open, and a terrible thought hit him. Epiphanically. This was King's Cross, he suddenly saw, notorious for its ladies of the night trade, a place where he had, one late evening, been asked the time by a prosthetic-legged girl in hot pants and then invited to "come home" with her. Needless to say, he'd run away faster than Usain Bolt. And here he was again. So *that* was what the whole Saint Mary's Gardens charade had been about. He had simply being the mark for a sex snatch.

"No, no, puh-*lease* no," he screamed clutching his wallet with one hand, and the black cab's door handle with the other, but to no avail. Bert, the cabbie who was evidently Gabi's pimp, removed James's hand with little difficulty and drove off, leaving him at her mercy.

"*Liebchen, Liebchen, mach nicht so viel Aufhebens* (Sweetie, sweetie, don't make such a fuss)," she whispered in his ear as he quivered on the pavement. Not that he'd have been able to make enough of a fuss to scarper pronto even if he'd wanted. Not with that man-like grip on both of his elbows as she steered him through the door. So in true Cockburn fashion, he gave up and, once inside her apartment and, laid out on some sort of a bed, succumbed again to the Valium.

~ * ~

James emerged from his drug-induced sleep maybe an hour later. For once he had lost interest in the precise time. As usual, however, he needed to ensure that upon awakening from unsettling dreams—James had always had unsettling dreams—he hadn't turned into a monster dung beetle like poor old Gregor Samsa in Kafka's *Metamorphosis*. To this end, he patted himself all over and was relieved to discover no hard carapace or peculiar appendages instead of legs. So far so good. Next step, open eyes. At which, he normally saw a white-going-on-grey ceiling up top and, by swiveling his head to left and right, a bedside table on one side, and a wardrobe on the other. His bedroom.

Unsurprisingly, when he did not see any of those familiar things, he gurgled ingressively. Great, so he wasn't a dung beetle, but he wasn't at home either so where the hell *was* he? The ceiling was a lemony colour and, as he craned his neck, the room was furnished with armchairs, a sofa, a mahogany escritoire littered with papers, and windows with flowery chintz curtains. He rapidly closed his eyes again and gurgled ingressively some more, digging and digging into a short-term memory that was unreliable at the best of times. No luck on the initial foray therefore. But then, on the second or third time around, he had it. The app, the cab, King's Cross, the whore called... what was her name again? Gobi, some name like that.

"Aaaagh," he said, rechecking his body to make sure it wasn't naked. But no, all clothes on. And, when he finally found it in his jacket pocket, his wallet was still intact. Furthermore, when he checked its contents—two twenties, one tenner, and three fivers—were still there, too. So, he concluded with some relief, he had been neither sexually exploited *nor* robbed. Mind you, he reflected, what kind of a whore was it who would have bothered having sex with a punter *before* stealing his money. So much easier just to take the cash and do a runner. But seeing as neither of those scenarios appeared to have obtained, what the hell *had* happened? He could only assume he was in the hands of some ethical kind of a whore who'd allowed him to sleep before she ravished him and demanded payment. One who believed in fair trade.

By then, James was gurgling ingressively so hard his throat hurt.

"Sleep well, *Liebchen*?" said a voice behind the mini-futon he must have nodded off on.

With some difficulty, and a lot of trepidation, he twisted his head around and this time the short-term memory hit the bull's eye with its first shot.

"*Guh*-Gabi?"

"The same, *Liebchen*. A glass of water? A cup of tea? Something stronger? I have a nice Pilsner."

Hiatus while James struggled and failed in the attempt not to verbalize his whore suspicions. Tact had never been his strongest suit. Foot in the mouth was his more usual style.

"Suh-so, you're nuh-not a huh-whore," he therefore said when the hiatus was over.

But, to give her due credit, despite the marginally raised eyebrows, Gabi just laughed.

"An easy mistake to make, I suppose," she said. "For one of your imagination. Now...the water? The tea? The Pilsner?

"Puh-Pilsner," said James, levering himself up on his elbows and ferreting in his pockets for the roll-up equipment he'd been toying with back in Queen Mary's Gardens in some other lifetime. "Mind if I smoke?"

"Feel free," said Gabi, eyeing his Blue Drum pouch and Rizla papers when he finally located them. "You could make me one, too?"

Then she was gone into some other part of what he took to be her apartment. While she was away, he wondered what she'd meant by the imagination comment. What did *she* know about his imagination and, more pertinently, *how* she did she know about it? Curiouser and curiouser this was all becoming. Scarily curiouser. Nonetheless, with fumbling fingers, he made them both a roll-up.

"*Also, Herr Doktor* Cockburn, here is your Pilsner," Gabi said on her return. Toting a silver salver on which stood two Bavarian-type *Steins* decorated with little figurines and sporting pewter lids with thumb levers.

There followed a flabbergasted hiatus, much longer than the last one, during which James's mouth dropped open much like that of a baby bird wanting dinner from its mother. *Herr Doktor* Cockburn? How did she...? He considered his chances of escape from this evident Lorelei. Tear apart the chintz curtains and leap through the window. But what if we were on the tenth floor? Knock her over and sprint for the door? Fat chance. The Lorelei was stronger and much more athletic than him. Mind you, so were most people. James had never done a day's exercise in his life, considering it ungentlemanly. Instead of undertaking such potentially life-saving, but clearly impossible measures, therefore, he merely remained seated and twitched spastically. No way of fixing *this* button torn from his jacket.

The Lorelei watched on unperturbed as she laid the *Steins* on a glass-topped coffee table between the futon and the armchair she was about to sit in.

"You have made my cigarette?" she asked when the seating was complete. Crossing the long tanned legs beneath the purple plush terry robe she must have changed into while he'd been asleep. He hadn't noticed it before. But that was James all over. How many times had Pauline—his ex—berated him for not noticing the latest addition to her well-stuffed wardrobe? For not noticing her newest perfume, for not noticing her latest article in *American Studies*, for not noticing *her*. As sensitive as a toilet seat, right? Too busy scribbling the silly stories no respectable publisher would touch with a barge pole.

James took a long, deep breath and tossed the cigarette onto the coffee table.

"Thanks," said the Rhine maiden, re-rolling the tobacco far more expertly than James had been able—you know how it is with Germans, how they love perfection—then, once satisfied, lighting up both cigarettes with a bronze-finish Dunhill, inhaling with satisfaction and blowing the smoke at the primrose ceiling.

"You may be wondering how I know your name," she added, thumbing the lid of her Stein and taking a long draught of the Pilsner.

James twitched some more, although this time less spastically. Amazing what the combination of Pilsner and nicotine could do for a person. Unless his drink had been spiked, of course. Whatever the reason, he made bold enough to say, "Actually, yes. It had crossed my mind."

Crossed his mind? It had infected his whole being from toes to hippocampus.

~ * ~

There were two reasons for Gabi knowing who James Cockburn was. The first was the impact he had unwittingly made during his brief spell teaching the genre-bending literature course he'd invented for the final-year programme at Heidelberg, which was apparently remembered with such enthusiasm by his alumni that the Cockburn prize was now awarded to the most successful student on the course. To James, it had seemed logical enough to dissociate people like Joyce, Beckett, Vonnegut, Calvino, Eliot, Pynchon, Sterne et al from the usual constipating classifications (Modernists, Postmodernists etc.) imposed on them by the lit crit industry, lump them all together, and set them free of their constraints. Not that his efforts had been much appreciated by the stuffed shirts running the department. *Very* sniffy they'd been. Particularly when he'd added in Paul Simon and Bob Dylan songs—played at full volume in class—and claimed them to be as poetic as the output of "proper" poets. But, according to Gabi, student power had won the day, such that the module had become so oversubscribed after he left, it had become a magnet for students from all over Germany, and the stuffed shirts had been forced to "stick their prejudices up their arses," as Gabi put it.

James blinked at this news. Bizarre indeed it was to learn of his unknown reputation in a foreign land. Like the revelation of some secret life he had never knowingly led. He blinked even harder when Gabi told him she herself now taught and loved the course. It had saved her from years of repetitious academic tedium, she said, while rolling two more cigarettes, this time to top-notch German standards.

"I owe you so much, Doctor Cockburn," she said, lighting the roll-ups for both of them then passing his over. "Thank you."

"*Bitte schön,*" James said. "I had no idea that..."

Gabi placed a forefinger over her lips and shook her head before moving on to her second reason for not only knowing his name but, with Internet assistance, also tracking him down to London.

"*Internet* assistance?" he said. Apoplectically. Again thinking Facebook, Cambridge Analytica and stolen IDs.

Gabi shrugged. "It wasn't easy. You are very secretive person, James. But even you cannot hide completely. Not when you are out there as an author. No email details for you, of course. But your publisher had one. He also had a home address for you and—"

"You've been in contact with *him*. I told him under no circumstances to divulge…" said James, with reference to the sole (vanity) publisher who'd been prepared to handle his manuscripts in exchange for five hundred pounds each.

"You would be surprised what a little charm and a few euros can achieve, James."

He dropped his head into his heads and kneaded it, almost wishing Gabi *had* been a whore. Better that than a stalker who had evidently studied his habitual haunts from a safe distance then finally pounced. She talked on, however, as he continued with the kneading, telling him how she had been saved by not only his genre-bending course, but also the novels he'd written since. How they broke fresh ground in a fiction industry so paralysed by mindless mediocrity, it only dared publish books it knew it could sell. Crime books were churned out by the millions. *Any* book with "girl" on the title page was a sure fire winner. Then there were the *Eighty Shades of Beige* copycats. Nothing to make a reader think, though. Until she'd found one of James's, that was. How it had ever got published she had no idea but, like his genre-bender course, it had saved her life.

"It spoke to me," she said, stubbing out her cigarette, "of things I had never fully considered. Straightforward language, no frills, some laughs along the way, storyline all over the place, bits of magic and the paranormal, but underlying all that, truths about what it's like to be human and live as a human."

Lifting his head from the kneading, James stared at her. This was the first time he'd had feedback from a reader. Judging from the paltry sums on his very occasional royalty statements, he'd always assumed he didn't have any readers. Except for Pauline, that was. But she, on sufferance, had only ever skimmed through one of his three books before declaring it "unliterary and stultifying in the nth degree," and swearing never to read another.

"And you've come all this way just to..." he said, suspicious of such flattery.

"Meet you in person," Gabi confirmed. "A fill-up of the Pilsner perhaps?"

He nodded and went back to the head kneading. Trying, with little success, to make sense of the last few hours. How many hours since he'd been sitting quietly in Queen Mary's Gardens minding his own business, he couldn't be sure. He wasn't even sure it was the same day as the light began to leak away from the sky outside the chintz-curtained windows, and the night drew in.

Three

At seven minutes past nine—James had begun to take an interest in time again—he told Gabi he'd like to go home, but she wouldn't hear of it.

"After I have come all this way to find you? There are so many things I still wish to say."

"Couldn't you perhaps say them tomorrow? We could meet up at The Rose Garden again. I won't run away, promise," he said, although that was precisely what he intended. His big brother William, the painter of dystopian abstract nudes, had a house in St Ives where he'd told James he could stay if he ever fancied a visit. Meet the family for the first time, take a look at the dystopian abstract nudes, that kind of thing. Just a question of hopping on a train at Paddington and, bingo, he'd be gone to where Gabi would never find him, however clever a stalker she was. *If* her tale of academic/literary detection was true, of course, which he was beginning to doubt. A few euros and some batting of eyelashes to persuade Art Swenson, his small-time "independent publisher" to hand over James's details to a complete stranger? James didn't think so. Art might not have been the *most* honest broker on the planet, but even he had a reputation of sorts to think of.

Gabi wasn't buying such delaying tactics, though. Even when James protested she couldn't keep him prisoner, she just laughed.

"You are not my *prisoner*, James. You are my new best friend. And in my life, I have had very few best friends. *Very* few," she said, the hint of a tear appearing in the canthus of her right eye. "Could we not at least have dinner together tonight? I know of a decent place off the Tottenham Court Road."

James sighed as the Tyranny of Niceness syndrome raised its ugly head, yet again. Maybe Gabi *was* a fraud, or just a very good actress. Or—just maybe—she was on the level and really did need his friendship. He'd never been good when it came to distinguishing the truths of human behaviour, never been able fully to delve beneath the surface patina to the inner person and trust his findings. One way or another, that's what his three novels had been all about. Maybe Gabi had spotted that. Maybe that's why she liked them. Plus, it was also true he was hungry. Unsurprising, seeing he'd eaten nothing since the apple whose core he'd chucked at either the first of two magpies or the same magpie seen twice. That and a few morsels of cherry cake. So it was that, as so often in his life and to his chagrin, he relented.

"Oh, all right then. But after the meal, I go home, okay?"

Gabi's face lit up like a child's at Christmas, and next thing he knew she was out of her armchair and planting the mother of all kisses on his right cheek.

"You are a good man," she said, pulling back and staring into his eyes when the kissing was over.

No answer to the going home question though, now or ever. Just a lot of app prodding at her smartphone to reserve a table at Chez Antoine and book another cab to take them there.

When she was satisfied with those arrangements, she hurried off to change into her "going out" clothes, calling over her shoulder as she went, "No trying to escape now, or I will app the police to find you." Her laughter trailed after her into what he assumed to be her bedroom.

James sank back onto his futon and shook his head at his own naïveté. When would he *ever* learn?

~ * ~

Chez Antoine was a faux chic joint, and the waiters evidently diplomates of some *École Supériere de L'Hauteur*. A person had to wonder about French restaurateurs, didn't he? Why they bothered opening London restaurants when they treated their customers with the sort of disdain a liege lord might when faced with a peasant. Mind you, James reflected, maybe that was precisely *why* British eaters patronized French restaurants with such eagerness. For the same reason they went to Madame Whiplash in Soho for a revitalising dose of flagellation. The waiter was a snooty boots called Jules, who must have graduated top of his class on the Contempt and Arrogance modules. He sported slicked-back hair plastered to his head, and a little pencil moustache beneath which the mouth was twisted into a perpetually pained pout.

"*Bonsoir*," he grunted, wafting a hand at their table in a remote corner of the eatery, then turning his back on them while flicking dust off the white napkin over his shoulder. It was another fifteen minutes before he reappeared to enquire what they might like to eat. Which wasn't an easy question to answer, because they hadn't been graced with menus.

Jules shrugged Gallically, sighed, and pointed at a blackboard so far away it was impossible to decipher what was written on it, raising his eyebrows and rolling his eyes as James and Gabi squinted into the distance.

"*Et alors*?" he said after maybe five minutes of this. That was the other thing with Jules. To add local colour *and* ensure clients hadn't a clue what he was on about and therefore feel inferior, he spoke only French. Mind you, James couldn't entirely blame him for that. Brits didn't have the finest reputation as polyglots when overseas, did they? Shout loud enough in English, and bally foreigners will eventually understand you, was the idea they'd had since colonial times. Fortunately, Gabi was fluent in the tongue, however, and even James managed the occasional *merci beaucoup*, albeit badly pronounced, to judge from Jules's sneer after he was obliged to read out the evening's dishes for them, which he did at a hundred miles a minute in some sort of slurred idiolectal argot, obliging even Gabi to ask for a repeat performance only more slowly this time. Jules did as requested but much in the manner of Jacques Tati addressing the two dumbest pupils in his class.

*Any*way, what with one thing and another, it was half an hour before Gabi and James were able to share their entrée of *escargots à la bourguignonne,* and a further fifteen minutes after that, before James's *agneau à point* with frites and peas and Gabi's beef *roulade* (also with frites and peas) arrived—in both cases to the accompaniment of the sorts of nose and moustache twitches from Jules that suggested their choice of foodstuffs was poor going on execrable.

Still they braved all this, and Gabi even found it amusing. "*Die Franzosen, nicht wahr?* (The French, eh?)," she giggled. "This is why I come here. For the performance."

James liked her for that.

And what did they talk about as Jules skulked around disapprovingly? All manner of things. Books again, obviously. James's in particular, over which Gabi poured so many eulogies, he was obliged to change the subject to critical issues of the day, on which they found themselves of very similar minds. That the madmen in the White House and the Kremlin deserved to be strung up by their testicles, and all the Brexiteers in the Tory Cabinet be thrown in the stocks in Parliament Square and have rotten eggs thrown at them, for example, they both agreed. It is always heartening when you see eye to eye with a person on thorny political issues of the day that might otherwise lead to hostility. Ditto for religion, of course, and James was relieved to discover Gabi, like him, was of the opinion God, Allah, and all other deities should be abolished if world peace were ever to be achieved. And so on and on they talked, the conversation oiled by the two bottles of Châteauneuf-du-Pape of which even Jules seemed to approve. *In vino veritas*, as they say. By the time they came to the coffee, fruit, cheese, and cognac course, they were relaxed enough to move on to personal histories, a topic James normally eschewed much as he might the plague. But as well as being a fan of his books—or perhaps because of it—Gabi was a willing listener, so for once he broke his own lifelong rule.

"You poor boy," said Gabi when he told her about Mater and Pater, the nannies, the boarding schools from age eleven, and his subsequent string of unsuccessful relationships, including the one with Pauline, who had always yawned if he ever dared speak about himself instead of her.

"Get over it and move on," was Pauline's favourite line on such occasions, looking at the time on her yellow smart watch before claiming an urgent appointment.

"Bitch," was Gabi's gratifying reaction to this confession.

Mind you, she hadn't had a much better a time of it herself, intelligence, good looks and the best bottom James had ever seen in Queen Mary's Gardens, apparently not having led to the sorts of happiness he would have expected. Quite the opposite, in fact. Why? Because none of the men Gabi had known liked her being more intelligent than them and were only interested in taking her clothes off, a lesson she'd learnt early in life back in Berlin. Never, therefore, had she trusted herself to anyone except a fellow student called Wolfgang who, after a tortuous and unconsummated relationship, had confessed he preferred boys, anyway.

"All very frustrating," she said, sipping at her Hennessy VSOP, reaching over to take James's hand, and staring at him meaningfully with her azure eyes.

James wouldn't have admitted to his heart having melted exactly, but it certainly missed the odd beat. Furthermore, any thoughts of going home or escaping to St Ives appeared to have flown out of the window.

"You poor girl," he was saying as Jules materialised from wherever he'd been hiding and, with a languid hand, dropped the bill onto their table. It came to a hundred and forty-five pounds and eighty-six pence, at which James recoiled.

"Holy *shit*," he said in the manner that had caused Pauline repeatedly to condemn him as a "mean bastard."

Gabi appeared unmoved, though. Just slid her plastic into the card machine Jules thrust onto the table and punched in the numbers that would enable payment, including the obligatory gratuity. Jules even managed what, for him, must have counted as a smile, although it came out as more of a leer.

Then she took to thumbing at her phone to order the cab that would take them home. To *her* home, that was. James had pretty much forgotten about his.

~ * ~

The thing James had *not* confessed to Gabi in their personal history swap session was that he wasn't very good at sex, as frequently pointed out by Pauline. Mind you, she wasn't the only one. There hadn't been all that many others down the years, but none had actually congratulated him on his performance. This was no American Psycho we were talking about. It wasn't that he couldn't do it at all. It was just that it had always been something of a disappointment for him as much as his partner, especially in the foreplay department. Why? Well, for a whole host of reasons, self-consciousness pretty much up there at top of the list. As mentioned (see above), he was no Brad Pitt and had never exercised in his life, so the body wasn't anything to write home about. No big biceps or quads or six packs or anything like that, and he only weighed a little over nine stone. These were things women noticed. It was all very well for *them* to moan about being held up as sex objects, but did anybody ever stop to think about the fate of the puny bloke? Of course, they didn't.

Anyway, there was that to take into account. But there were other things too. Knowing the person's mind, *speaking* to them at length before having sex with them, had always been a priority for James such that, contrary to the commonly accepted belief that any stud worth his salt got an erection simply by *seeing* a naked woman, James didn't. Which didn't help. Not that it ran in the family, because brother William not only painted his dystopian abstract nudes but also boasted of having reckless sex with them, "family or no bloody family." Not James though. He just wasn't dominant enough in that regard. Put simply, there was no way he could *know* a potential lover's mind—which he needed to—simply by looking at her tits and ass, and that tended to be a bit of a downer, so to speak.

Then there was the act itself, always assuming he could get to that stage. In his humble (and limited) experience, the only two women he'd more or less managed to perform with expected *him* to do all the work. All they thought *they* had to do was lie down naked in front of him, spread their legs a bit, and hey, presto, he'd pounce on them and take his pleasure. Well, that didn't work. James had even slept—i.e. shut his eyes and gone to sleep—with a number of subsequently confused women who, thereafter, accused him of damaging their egos and refused ever to see him again. Understandably, he supposed.

So that was a confession he did *not* make to Gabi. Would you have? I don't think so. Nonetheless, during the cab ride home, he began to sense the strangest of sensations in her regard. Not lust, nothing as smutty as that. Desire, for want of a better word, a for him peculiar wish to be closer to her. No stiffy in his pants or anything, just a feeling of belonging. From the way she held his hand, he suspected she might be feeling the same way, too. Love at first sight? Well, maybe.

Whatever it was, it manifested itself very quickly when they arrived back at Gabi's apartment, and she took his hand and led him into her bedroom where she helped him as he fumbled with his clothes, then plonked him supine onto the bed before stripping herself. Not a word spoken between them, just straight down to business and, for the very first time, James forgot his hang-ups, and it worked like a dream. So much so that they did it all over again—twice—before exhaustion took over. Why? Because the act was reciprocal, that was why. As he explained at some length to Gabi afterwards, and she agreed, it had been as much a cerebral experience as a physical one, the two normally distinct categories having magically merged.

"Minds *and* bodies together," he said, on the very cusp of asking her to marry him. He didn't though.

And thus ended the most surreal day of James Cockburn's life to date. So much packed into so little time. Time that shrank and shrank as his eyes closed until it seemed like no more than a disconnected haze. Then he was asleep and, whoosh! just like that, the day was gone.

Four

For the following weeks—two weeks, four weeks, he was no longer counting—James was magically, blissfully, happy. And let's be clear, James didn't use clichés like "magical," "blissful," or "happy" easily. No such word had ever appeared in any of his books because his characters, mainly him in disguise, were barely ever even cheerful. But then, you didn't meet many jolly existentialists, did you? Something of an oxymoron *that* would have been, James reckoned, so he'd stuck to the straightforward moody blue types like him, gloomy blokes who never even chuckled. Gobsmacked he was, therefore, suddenly to find himself en*joying* things without ever asking why or wondering what retribution he would receive as a result. It was like bundling up all his old clothes, throwing them in the river, and finding himself wearing brand new ones. Like wiping the slate clean and starting afresh. Like having a transfusion of new blood. Like any other hackneyed analogy he could think of. In short, he was in love in precisely the way portrayed in all the pop songs he had previously ridiculed. Cupid's arrow, and love the many splendoured thing, and all that. So, goodbye cynicism, hello optimism. No more the nightmares in which he is pursued by inchoate cackling demons intent on scooping out his entrails and eating them. Instead, sweet nocturnal rapture from which he awoke smiling gormlessly as Gabi gave him head massages. For yes, he had Airbnb-rented his basement hovel in Hackney, moved in with her, and settled to a life of previously unthinkable domestic rapture. Walks in Queen Mary's Gardens to celebrate the birth of their bond, rowing little boats on the Serpentine, eating so regularly at Chez Antoine even Jules started being polite to them. At the risk of further banality, it was all far too good to be true. So overwhelmed was he that James had even stopped counting magpies.

"*Liebchen, bist du glücklich*? (Darling, are you happy?)" Gabi would whisper in his ear every night in the new king size bed they'd bought, courtesy of the Airbnb money.

"Deliriously," he would whisper back, and meaning it. "I've never been happier in my life." Which was true (see above).

"And you love me?" she would ask.

"More than anything on earth."

"*Wunderbar.*"

And indeed it was wonderful, wonderful and wond*rous*. He wanted it to last forever.

"Kiss me," she would say.

At which, he would wink knowingly.

"Where?" he would say with his new sex-machine grin.

"Anyplace you want, honeychile," she would reply in what she thought of as her Mississippi accent.

And there they would be, at it all over again. Whoever wrote the Kama Sutra would have been amazed. James certainly was.

~ * ~

It wasn't until his brother William, the painter of dystopian abstract nudes, called one day saying he'd just landed his very first exhibition down in St Ives, and inviting his brother to the show that the bliss morphed into the kind of angst James had portrayed in his second book *The Kiss of Death*, in which an anti-hero called Winston McBride is held against his will by a harridan called Mathilde Dunoir in what James had conceived of as an imaginatively romantic reworking of the Stockholm Syndrome. It was the pink fit Gabi threw when he told her of William's invitation that revived this all-but-buried fear of the female as dominatrix.

And why did he make this apparently extreme connection? Because Gabi had reacted with such extremity herself to the idea of him going off to St Ives alone, that was why. Even when he said she could come along too, he was sure William would love to meet her, she took to stomping up and down the King's Cross apartment tugging at her hair ululating, "*Nein, nein, nein,* you are mine, mine, mine." You can imagine his concern as the relationship to which he'd devoted his recent life suddenly took this ugly turn. Mind you, as he looked back over the last few weeks since the Rose Garden encounter, it began to make a terrible sense. Yes, he and Gabi had become an indissoluble item, and yes, they'd had fabulous sex, but had he ever been alone or spent solo time in anybody else's company in those weeks? Answer, no. When he looked back, Gabi had always been there, chaperoning him about wherever he went. Not that he'd complained, mind you. So much under her spell was he, he hadn't even noticed. But now, as she rampaged around the apartment like a thwarted *Gauleiter,* the possibility of a terrible truth dawned. Not the Stockholm Syndrome in its original form of literal kidnapping followed by captor worship, something much more subtle, but equally ensnaring, something he, like Winston McBride, had confused with love.

"Even if you don't come, I'd only be away for a day or two, and he is my brother, after all," he protested, but to no avail as Gabi took to grinding her teeth and muttering Germanic imprecations even he couldn't translate. Okay, the *Scheißkopf* was easy enough, but whatever else that followed in some impenetrable dialect wasn't.

"Look, *Liebchen,* let's be sensible about this," he tried, but her once lovely face had morphed into a mask of horror, not unlike the one in Munch's *Der Schrei,* except hers included ghastly grimaces as she stalked about the room drawing curtains and slamming down shutters. James was pretty terrified. What if she took to locking the doors to ensure he couldn't escape?

But then, only moments later, it was all over, and Gabi was on her knees pulling at her hair, weeping, and begging forgiveness.

"I am soooo sorry," she spluttered between bouts of body-racking sobs.

"Okay, it's...okay," he lied, holding up both palms irenically.

"It...is...*not*...O-fucking-K. Nothing with me is okay. You poor, poor man that you should know me," she added, calming a little while blatting her hands on the carpet. "I am a bad, *bad* girl."

"Cup of tea, perhaps?" he said, following the peculiarly British belief that tea contains properties capable of resolving all crises.

"Tea," she agreed, staggering to her feet. "Tea."

It was as he was off in the kitchen quivering while watching a kettle that seemed unprepared to boil that thin rays of light began to re-enter the apartment from what he assumed were re-opened shutters, and he sensed Gabi behind him. Hopefully not with a raised frying pan in her hand.

"Won't be a mo," he said, taking an unnatural interest in the contents of the teacup cupboard. "Two sugars as usual?"

"Three. With brandy."

"You're sure that would be a good idea, Gabi?"

"*Weinbrand*," she insisted, ferreting in the booze cupboard and plonking the bottle in front of him on the polished-tile kitchen island surface.

"Okay, fine. As you wish. Tea with brandy coming right up," he said as the reluctant kettle finally boiled, and he poured the water onto the Assam leaves in the pot. "Just needs a couple of minutes to brew."

Funny things rituals, aren't they? Soothing even in the midst of chaos. That was the outcome of this dramatic episode, anyway. By the time the two of them were sitting side by side on the white sofa sipping at their cuppas, they could have been Mister and Missus Ordinary after a tiring day at work. They weren't though. Of course, they weren't. Talk about elephants in rooms.

"Fuh-feeling better, *Luh-Liebchen*?" James said in the calmest voice he could muster.

Gabi laughed the way a hangee might on her way to the gallows. She had broken into a cold sweat all over. But, at least, she was more or less coherent.

"Better than what?"

"Than before. When you were..."

"Out of my *mind*?"

James checked his tea. Made sure it was satisfactorily stirred.

"Well?" said Gabi, swilling her cup down in one gulp and refilling it from the brandy bottle.

"You were clearly a little on edge."

"Edge. *Edge*? I was out of my fucking *mind*. I never know when it is going to happen. But it *happens*."

Hello elephant.

~ * ~

Tentatively, when the brandy had calmed her a little, James asked Gabi for more details of the "it" that kept happening out of the blue. What with his own hang-ups of one kind or another, he was not the person best placed to consult on matters of mental health and was no believer in talking cures, but even he couldn't let such an episode slip by without comment.

"You've no idea what causes it?" he said. "What the trigger is?"

Not the subtlest of questions. A bit like a shrink asking an analysand what was the matter with him, to which the only rational answer was, "That's what I came here to find out, you dickhead." But Gabi seemed grateful nonetheless.

"You are a kind man," she told him in a voice so small he could barely make out her words.

Then came the history she'd explained to more Freudians and other analysts than she could remember, none of whom had been able to suggest a cure. Nods of sympathy as they excavated the depths of her mind until the clocks on their desks ticked around to the end of their fifty-minute sessions, but, as she put it, "They might just as well have told me they were sorry, but I was nuts, and there was nothing they could do about it."

"Okay, there were pills I could have taken," she added, reaching again for the brandy bottle, "but all pills come with side effects sometimes worse than the bloody symptoms."

"I know," James said, at which she stared at him and frowned.

"You *do*?"

So he told her about the pills he'd been given to sort out his partial Tourette's and the borderline bipolarity he had vicariously explored in his novels, which was one of the reasons Pauline had ridiculed his writing as "self-obsessed trash" and told him to stop beating himself up, "draw a line" under his fatuous family, and "get a life." Which advice was about as helpful as the pills he was prescribed to stop the nightmares and, instead, just gave him different ones.

He guessed it was this confession that paved the way for Gabi to tell him her story. Nothing like a fellow sufferer when it comes to the empathy shrinks cannot show because they are meant to be the bastions of sanity. And once she'd recounted it, he wasn't surprised at the difficulties she'd later suffered. After all, it can't have been easy to be have been born in Lichtenberg, East Berlin in 1980, the child of a Stasi sergeant father and his mousey wife. To have been indoctrinated in communist dogma day in day out and obliged to report on any friends whose parents or siblings appeared to be straying from the state's requirements when you were a mere child. Even less easy— although it was all you had ever wanted—to run away in 1992 through the now liberated Checkpoint Charlie, and never again to have anything to do with the both loved and hated family you had left behind. Understandable, but not without consequences of deep guilt when you were adopted by a new family in Zehlendorf, West Berlin, offered the best education available, and for years, learned no longer to care if your birth parents and brothers were dead or alive. Who truly to love, who truly to hate? Such was the conundrum Gabi thought she'd mastered and overcome until the "bad girl" feelings began in her late teens, and the need to dominate and control relationships had surfaced as unwelcome guests during her postgraduate days at the *Freie Universität* in Berlin. Needless to say, none of those relationships had survived. A pretty girl but crazy became her reputation.

"I'm sorry," James said. And he was. At least Mater and Pater had just been mainly absent from his life. Tricky in its own way that had been, leaving him feeling unloved and unwanted by the very people who should have been the most supportive. But he imagined even that was easier to deal with than state-sponsored domestic ideological abuse necessitating escape from those who had spawned you. When you were only twelve. Mind you, he had also heard similar stories during his time in Heidelberg. From a different, younger, generation than Gabi, of course, but in Germany there lingered the aftertaste of both the repercussions of World War Two and, especially in the south east, of fascism itself. What of the fathers and grandfathers who had willingly played their part in those upheavals? This was a question to which a number of his students had received no satisfactory answers and were still puzzling over.

It was after James recounted some of these tales that Gabi burst into more tears and fell on his neck. He cuddled her and meant it.

"Another cup of tea, perhaps?" he said when the cuddling was more or less over.

"You bloody English with your tea," said Gabi. But she was laughing, and he was heartened to see it.

Then, to his relief, she finger-combed through her tangled hair and began asking him about William and St Ives.

"And you think he would really not mind if I came, too?" she said after James admitted he'd never been to St Ives but had heard it was fun and was sure William would be only too pleased to meet her, but she'd need to take her strongest chastity belt with a specially enhanced Yale padlock.

That made her laugh, and James was glad to hear it.

"So, I will book the tickets," said Gabi, thumbing at her phone for the Trainline app.

Five

The trip from Paddington Station down to St Ives for their overnight stay with William went fine. There had been no more schizo outbursts in the last few days and Gabi seemed to enjoy the ride. Peering out of the window and expressing her astonishment that England had more fields and woods and nature than she ever could have imagined from the vantage point of King's Cross.

"Green and pleasant land," James told her.

She liked St Ives, too. Clean beaches with California-type surfers on the one hand, and long haired beardy-weirdy artist folk strolling the streets on the other, both groups getting on surprisingly well together. Having never before visited the place, even James was amazed after the anonymity of London.

"Like some foreign country," Gabi commented.

"Well, I guess it is really. Or was. Used to have its own language, a bit like Celtic or Breton. And its own parliament. Some folk down here want it back."

"Like the Scottish and the Welsh and the Northern Irish."

"Exactly."

"For me, this is a good idea."

James nodded. Who in their right mind would want to remain part of a United Kingdom governed by the Brexit clowns in London and, in Cornwall's case, pay nineteen million pounds a year in rents to its royal duke? Only a madman. Gabi was right, and he loved her the more for her assessment.

He also appreciated the way she handled big brother William, his partner Stephanie, and their two children, eleven year-old Ernest, who was *very* earnest, and six year-old Georgina, who was very boisterous and girly. Nobody would have suspected for a minute the dark side of Gabi's mind as she laughed and played with these two brats. The private face and the public face, right? James's brother, sister-in-law, nephew and niece only ever saw the public one. Gabi could be a charmer as he knew only too well.

"A good-un you've got there, little bro," William told him in the Cornish brogue he'd assumed the better to fit into his adopted homeland. "Better than the Pauline bint by a country mile."

James shrugged self-deprecatingly as he had done with his big brother since they were kids, there being no mileage in ever pretending any sort of equality, let alone superiority, with William unless he wanted a duffing up when the latest nanny wasn't looking.

"Just got lucky," he said.

"Very. Nice bod, too. Reckon she'd pose for me?" Subtext: "Reckon she'd screw me?"

James splayed his palms and shrugged again. "Probably not. We're only here a couple of days, so…"

"Pity," said William. "How's the latest book going?"

"Oh, you know, slowly."

"Same old James."

~ * ~

William's dystopian abstract nudes in his section of the exhibition of recent work by local artists entitled The Shock of The Nude were, in James's opinion, atrocious. Especially, the two ten-foot tall ones painted directly onto a wall. The obese man was all purple, and the obese woman blue with hints of yellow, and both were posed to show depictions of their blubbery bottoms beneath which, through opened legs, their bent-over faces were girning gummily at each other. The piece was entitled "Frolicsome Fatties," and caused James's bowels to churn. Even Gabi, who had come with every intention of praise, turned an ominous shade of green, and snorted meaningfully. Several of the culture vultures standing behind her said pompously arty-farty things like, "Mmm, interesting," and "Just a smidgeon of the playful postmodern pastiche in-mixed with the aftertaste of cubism, eh?" But the majority agreed with James and Gabi, i.e. they were pretentious shite. One, a woman James judged to be in her late seventies, opined it was "viscerally vulgar" and deserved to be burnt off with a blowtorch, a view with which James fully concurred.

And the rest of William's oeuvre, which focused entirely on the dystopian female nude, wasn't any better. Anorexic nudes with scabies and iridescent pubes, nudes with nonagenarian skin hanging off them like ill-fitting underwear, Dali-esque melting clock-type nudes on the lavatory, pixelated nudes fiddling with their bulbous genitalia, page-three-type nudes with fabulous bodies but spiders' legs...and so on, all of them, however, with perfectly ordinary, almost photorealistic, faces. By the time Gabi and James reached the last one, they were wishing they'd come with supplies of anti-vomit pills.

"Yuck," said Gabi, for example.

"Christ on a bike," James was saying as William materialised ahead of them with a big grin on his bearded face. Being a forty-five year-old dedicated follower of foolish fashion, he also wore his greying hair tied up in a topknot.

"Well? What d'you think?" he said.

"Same old William," James said, at which he frowned.

"Which I am meant to interpret as *what*?"

"Unusual."

"Unusual and brilliant?"

"*Unwahrscheinlich*," said Gabi, shaking her head and leaving William in the dark because he didn't speak German, and, therefore, didn't know *unwahrscheinlich* could mean either "dubious" as a negative, or "incredible" as a positive. But he liked the sound of comment anyway and kept rolling it across his tongue. "Unforsheenblick" he kept saying over and over.

"A woman of excellent taste, your babe, little bro," he said when he'd stopped saying unforsheenblick. "You two fancy a snifter in the bar to celebrate?" he added, a furtive hand straying towards Gabi's fabulous bottom in its faded blue denim cutoffs.

"Not today, José," said James, gripping the hand and steering it back to its owner.

"Some other time," said Gabi, breaking her I-like-William code. "Why don't you go back to your family?"

Stephanie and the brats had been left outside the gallery in the "mini artists" Play Doh area.

"Spoilsports," said William, fiddling with his topknot.

"Up yours, big bro," were the last words James directed at William. Out of earshot, backwards over his shoulder as he steered Gabi away to safety.

~ * ~

It was on the train back to Paddington the following morning that Gabi dropped the beneficent public-face mask she'd been wearing for the duration of their stay, bar the gallery visit, and told James she thought William was not only a crap painter, but also, sick in the head.

"I wouldn't go *that* far," James said with a shrug. "He has his faults, of course. Who doesn't? He is obviously a crap painter, but sick in the head might be overstating it a bit."

"A guy who paints grotesque nude bodies with perfect faces, and he is *not* sick in the head? Some trouble *he* is going to get into."

James was momentarily distracted from Gabi's insights into his brother's psyche by needing to inform a fat woman plonking herself down into a seat opposite while still yacking into her smartphone she was in the wrong carriage; this was the silent one. Not that she paid any attention. Just went on yacking. You know how it is with smartphones, how they disconnect their users' sensoria from the outside world.

"What does he think he's *doing*?" Gabi went on. "Taking the piss from his models?"

"William was always a bit of a misogynist. Mother issues," James replied, scowling at the fat woman and pointing at the sign above her head saying this was the silent carriage and all phones had to be switched off.

The fat woman merely scowled back and went on yacking about a boob job she'd just had done that made her look ravishingly sexy. And this in *public*.

"Bloody *hell*," James was saying as, embarrassingly, *his* smartphone took to trilling in his pocket.

Before he hooked up with Gabi, James never carried a smartphone on the twin excuses he didn't know how they worked and didn't want to learn, seeing as they were only for braindead dorks with narcissus complexes, citing the madman in the White House as a fine example of the species. But, as with many other aspects of his life, he'd been persuaded it was high time he joined the twenty-first century. Soon, Gabi had said—confirming his own suspicions (see above)—money as we knew it would become obsolete, and he wouldn't be able to buy anything without a phone. No food, no wine, no tobacco, no taxi rides, no clothes...the list went on. So, unless he really *wanted* to carry on living like some Neanderthal, it was about time he bought one. To which advice, James had grudgingly succumbed, hence the refurbished Apple he carried but never used. Only two people had the number: Gabi and, on her insistence they stay in touch, William's long-suffering wife, Stephanie. And seeing as Gabi was sitting next to him blethering about how William was bonkers, this had to be Stephanie.

"Bollocks," he said.

Gabi just giggled, shrugged, and told him to let it go to voicemail. But, he didn't know how to work the voicemail and, breaking into a sweat, dragged the hated instrument from his pocket, gesticulated pointedly at the fat woman with the ace boob job, and headed for the door at the end of the carriage, through which he was pushing just as the phone stopped bleating.

"*Fuck*," he said, turning on his heels.

But then the phone took to quivering in his hand and bleating all over again the ringtone Gabi had set for him—an instrumental version of "Heartbreak Hotel" by Elvis Presley.

"Holy shit," he said, nonetheless swiping at the green icon saying Accept Call.

"Yes?" he then spat into the choked weepy sound coming through the speaker.

"Juh-Juh-*James*?" said Stephanie.

"Who *else* would it be?" he said, pretty much at the end of his rope.

Which was when he learned William was dead. And not in a good way. Nothing as simple as a cardiac arrest suffered from over-exuberant sex with one of his dystopian abstract nude models, the sort of thing a grieving family might regard as poetic justice but nonetheless recover from. No, no, nothing as relatively benign, as Stephanie explained in juddering monosyllables, for brother William had been decapitated with a scimitar in his studio while working on a new painting of dystopian nymphs masturbating. The head was missing but on the naked body were painted footprints and on a repeating loop secreted somewhere inside him played "These Boots Are Made For Walkin'" by Nancy Sinatra.

James was pretty shocked. And when he'd hung up—or clicked off or whatever it was people did with mobiles to shut them up—and hurried back to Gabi to give her the news, so was she. Well, shocked, but not all that surprised. Behind her appropriately chastened eyes lurked nonetheless one of her best told-you-so looks.

Six

Unsurprisingly, life changed big time after William Cockburn's demise. You know how it is when a close relative gets gruesomely offed, how hacks and paparazzi from all the most lurid red tops come skulking about outside your door wanting candid shots and intimate details. James and Gabi copped plenty of that. Mater and Pater *were* traced to their extortionately expensive home for the terminally doolally, but even the most intrepid of journos gave up on them fast. Not a lot of insider info were they going to be able to glean from parents who no longer knew they *had* children and believed themselves to be on a P&O liner permanently cruising the Indian Ocean. It was all down to James and Gabi, therefore. At the London end of things, anyway.

In St Ives, it was Stephanie who was plagued and suffered the nervous breakdown that persuaded James and Gabi to return to Cornwall and help out. Not that James had wanted to, not being much of the helping-out type, but Gabi said they had no option except to go back, so back they went. And it wasn't just the dirt-diggers of the press they had to confront. Obviously, enough of the local coppers had questions about William's background, and any salient peccadillos that might have had a bearing on his decapitation, and, critically, in the investigation, potential locations for his missing head. As if James had a clue where it was.

Mind you, it was no longer any use protesting his total ignorance on the matter after the postmortem discovery of the scribbled note stuffed up William's anal canal saying "It wOz JaMeS wOt DuNniT." That put the pussy right amongst the pigeons, notwithstanding the fact that James hadn't even seen his brother since The Shock of The Nude show. William, offended at not being pronounced brilliant, only unforsheenblick, presumably had called later saying he'd be busy at the studio all night, so not to expect him for dinner and hadn't even bothered to turn up at the station the following morning to wave James and Gabi goodbye. Now, this bloody note trying to blame the heinous act on his brother! Obviously left by the real killer as a diversionary tactic to take up police time while he—or more likely *she* given William's preference for abusing wild, wild dystopian abstract women—escaped scot free after wreaking her vengeance.

~ * ~

James didn't like crime fiction stories, which was why he'd never tried his hand at writing one. He found them repetitive and tedious across the range, from the quirky American PI with dope, drink and divorce problems—the three Ds as James called them—to the "true crime" police procedural stories. Even the greats like Miss Marbles, as he dubbed her, bored him, especially when translated to TV. How many variations on murder could there *be*? No more than half a dozen, James reckoned, so after the up-front corpse, writers had to fill their pages with *some*thing, ergo the whole charade of red herrings, culs de sac, misleadingly idyllic backgrounds, implied interpersonal sub-plots, or anything else to retain readers' attention. Were Holmes and Watson gay, for example? Would three-time divorcee and recovering alcoholic DCI Jimmy "Shoeshine" Johnson of Chattanooga PD derive sufficient acumen from his AA sessions to allow what was left of his brain to focus on the investigation, or would he succumb to his addiction—and his covert love affair with Sergeant Milly McDougal—in time to solve the case, or wouldn't he? Otherwise, the space got filled by supposedly expert scenes of autopsy lab, Y-section corpse analyses to discover what could be hidden in the vic's intestines or pubic hair follicles that might lead to the capture of its assailant. And we were supposed to be interested in all this? James didn't think so. Especially when it was the forty-fifth book in the same series with the same hero the author had written because he or she once hit the market big time, couldn't think of anything else to write about and wanted to keep the royalties coming. No wonder the publishing and film industries were currently so bereft of originality. Anyway, from his ivory sanctuary of critical wisdoms, that was James's beef about crime fiction novels. That and the absurd notion of the vicarious and cathartic relief a reader was supposed to expect from textual exposure to violent crime and its tidy resolution. Piffle, James reckoned, and being hauled in by the local constabulary as the prime suspect in his brother's murder, and held in custody overnight, did little to change his mind when it came to the real-life experience of law enforcement. If anything, it lowered, yet further, his already dismal estimation of the inflated version of police persons' intelligence quotients as peddled by the fiction industry.

The first question on DI Horace Skewes's mind the following morning was of course how the "It wOz JaMes wOt DuNniT" note got stuffed up William's arse hole in the first place, although even Skewes at least accepted it would have been nuts of James to have left such a self-inculpatory note there himself. Not that he was ruling out an insanity plea in his defence.

"Just don't go wastin' my time with *that* idea, sonny, cos' it won't get you *no*where, okay? You can *try* proving to me you're the most nutty person since Norman The Most Nutty Person On The Planet all you like, but it won't cut no ice with this copper, so you can forget diminished fucking responsibility as an excuse right now. Been around the block too many times on this job to fall for *that* one, haven't I?"

"Shouldn't I have a lawyer present?" said James, but Skewes ignored the objection, asking instead where James had been at the time of William's murder, a question James countered by asking when exactly that had been. To which he received no answer, seeing as Skewes was still waiting on the autopsy report in that regard. Instead, the DI pursued an investigative angle based on hearsay from The Shock of The Nude show, suggesting James had been envious of his brother's artistic success, after which there had been a falling out culminating in the words: "Up yours, big bro," before James and "his woman" had stalked off muttering to each other. Skewes had an "unnamable source," who would swear to having overheard this exchange.

James rebuffed this accusation by telling Skewes he couldn't give a rat's arse for William's painterly prowess, let alone have any wish to chop his head off in envy. Also, he didn't possess a scimitar and wouldn't know how to use one if he did.

Skewes pounced on this.

"Skimiter? How d'you know the murder weapon was a *skimiter*?" he said, leaning into the interview table to eyeball James with his fiercest eyeballing technique.

"Because his wife told me while I was on the train back to London, not having seen my brother since the previous afternoon."

"Bah, paff," said Skewes scribbling sinistrally at a yellow, lined, legal pad.

"It's the truth, Sergeant. Check the train tickets."

"Detective In*spec*tor."

"Detective Inspector. And if *I* were looking for a suspect, the first place I'd look would be at the nudes my brother painted. Many reasons for *them* being pissed off with him there would be. *Every* cause they would have to bear a grudge. Such pretty faces and then underneath them those *bodies*? You know William screwed *all* his models, don't you? Come to think of it, any one of them could have dunnit and put the blame on me. All you need to do is make a list of his dystopian abstract female nude models and check out each of the girls' background for violent crime. My money would be on the anorexic one with scabies and iridescent pubes."

DI Skewes scowled. "Don't tell me how to do my job, sunshine, all right? Also how'd you write 'dustoopanian' when it's at home?"

"Sorry, just trying to help," said James after spelling out 'dystopian' letter by letter.

"Says here you're a writer," said the copper, thumbing through a dog-eared photocopy of some official document or another.

"That's right."

"Of what?"

"Books."

Skewes screwed up his eyes and cracked his knuckles ominously. "And don't come the clever pants with me neither," he said.

"I wasn't. I write books as opposed to advertising copy or newspaper articles. Or..."

"Don't tell me pomes. I don't like pomes."

"That makes two of us. In any case, if poems were what I wrote, I'd have been described as a poet, wouldn't I?"

Skewes scowled again. James could tell the bloke was starting to dislike him, and he needed to be careful.

"What kinds of books?"

"Oh, you know, novels."

"*Novels* eh?" said Skewes, scribbling while hoisting a sneering eyebrow.

"Yes," said James, sensing the man to be the reader of only car maintenance manuals if he read at all. No point in any exegesis of his literary style therefore. Go down like a bowl of cold sick that would. What James needed ASAP was to get the hell out of there before he wound Skewes up any further.

"Now, *if* you've no more questions, detective inspector," he therefore said, "I should like to be on my way. You have already held me beyond the twenty-four hour legal limit and were you to wish to interview me further, I understand it would be my right to have my lawyer present."

Skewes scowled again but knew he was on a hiding to nothing where the law was concerned.

"Just don't leave town, okay," he said as if he were Wyatt Earp or someone.

And so it was that James finally emerged from the cop shop and got clutched by Gabi, who had mounted a protest vigil in the street outside for the duration of his stay in the cells.

"*Liebchen*, are you all right?" she cried while James did his best to appear calm, British, and stoical.

"It was nothing," he lied. "Still a few loose ends to tie up, though."

Like who *had* written the It wOz JaMes wOt duNniT note stuffed up William's bottom, for example.

~ * ~

James and Gabi returned post haste to the Cockburn residence at number forty-eight Salubrious Place where Stephanie was still caught up in her nervous breakdown, and journos were still lurking about disguised as fisherfolk. And these weren't just your local hacks. Amongst them mingled stringers from all the big London papers, plus radio and TV stations, many of them interviewing each other in order to come up with any new angle on the story that had caught the imagination of the nation. And not just in the regular media. It was also, obviously enough, all over the Twitterzone in which rabid tweeters of all ages were postulating their views on the appalling nature of William's "execution," which many were attributing to the work of either ISIS sleeper cells in places as diverse as the Isle of Skye and Folkestone, or to Russian hitmen under orders from the Kremlin. You know how it is with tweeters. How febrile their imaginations can be, as indeed were those of proper newshounds who should have known better, otherwise, there would not have been headlines like "Crazed Assassin On The Loose In Cornwall."

James and Gabi pushed their way through this media scrum with Gabi in the van looking fierce while James sidled along behind. Mercifully, Skewes had not yet released news of the "It wOz JaMes wOt duNniT" note and, even if he had, nobody would have recognized James as the James in question because Gabi had come prepared with a dog collar and cassock, telling anyone with the temerity to ask he was the local vicar.

Once over Stephanie's and the ex-William's threshold, however, James cast off his vestments and did his best to persuade his sister-in-law it was about time she stopped breaking down nervously, and faced up to the future, even employing such hackneyed clichés as, "time is a great healer", and "there are more fish in the sea" at which she took to headbanging a wall and wailing.

James looked to Gabi for assistance. It may well be, as he sometimes claimed, that women talked too much, but there were occasions on which their super-loquacity proved helpful, particularly when exchanged between each other, as was the case on this occasion. Within moments of Gabi throwing her arms around Stephanie, drawing her to her breast, and whispering a cascade of language into her ear, relative silence descended on number forty-eight Salubrious Place. Funny name for a street, right? But it's true. In St Ives, there is also one called Virgin Street, and another called Teetotal Street. Apparently, John Wesley had done a spot of Methodist preaching around town back in the eighteenth century, and some of his sillier ideas had taken root.

Anyway, once Stephanie had been sufficiently soothed, James stepped back into the breach with further platitudes about what a loving husband and father William must have been and how much Stephanie would miss him. This even though he hadn't seen his brother in years and knew full well of his serial philandering.

"Such a terrible loss to us all," he lied, as Gabi, who had only met him once, nodded dutifully. "Anything at all we can do. Such a *nice* man he seemed," she said, swallowing hard.

That was when Stephanie stopped being a frenetic head banger and went all steely and cold.

"He was a bastard," she said in her native Cornish twang. "A bastard who'd bonk anything in a skirt. Or better still, without one."

James adopted his mask of feigned astonishment. "My brother *William*?" he said.

"Yeah, your sodding brother Willy Arse."

"Dear, dear, so sorry to hear it. Still, he's left you with a nice little house and—"

"No...bloody...*MONEY*," said Stephanie reverting to manic mode in the bat of an eyelid. "Not much use even alive, he wasn't."

James gave her his fish-out-of-water look, which only served to exacerbate matters and cause Gabi to clutch Stephanie in another Teutonic bear hug as she took to blatting herself around the head with both flattened palms.

But Stephanie wasn't finished with the accusations. Through the head-blatting and blubbering emerged not only the story of William's inveterate meanness with money, of which, he never had enough because he was a crap painter, but also the tale of the pirate treasure trove buried in a secret cave beneath the cliffs of St Ives Bay. All filled with diamonds, and gold nuggets, and silver bars it was, William had told her. And he was the only one to know about it. But did he ever give *her* any of them? Like hell he did.

James sighed.

Furthermore, William wouldn't tell her where exactly it was. He'd taunted her year in and year out saying some day, when he was dead, she would learn the secret from a mysterious source, and then it would be all hers. James sighed again as Stephanie's frustration bubbled to the surface, and it took Gabi all her strength to hold on to her. William had been infamous since childhood for his pirate stories, but James had always laughed them off. That was William for you, the prize bullshitter who masked his never admitted insecurities behind as many fabulations as he could muster, a practice he had apparently maintained even in later years with his wife.

"Just one more of William's fantasies probably," he said in the vain hope of calming Stephanie, who repeated "*bast*ard" before adding, "Cheating *lying* bastard."

"Leave her to me," whispered Gabi, holding up an irenic palm as she led Stephanie to a sofa, sat her down, and patted her knees.

James wandered off into the kitchenette and peered out of a tiny unwashed window at the scruffy little gardenette outside, unbidden musings dripping into his mind. Sure enough William was a bullshitter, always had been...but...but what *if* this apparent fairy story contained some arcane element of truth? After all, the history of piracy in the waters between Cornwall and Brittany across the centuries was well documented, so hidden treasure troves weren't *entirely* out of the question. Maybe, William had just lit on the idea as an aspect of local colour that suited purposes known only to himself. But what if...?

Also what if—a terrible thought—in her desperation to learn the whereabouts of the fabled treasure, Stephanie's patience had finally snapped and...well...she'd ensured William *was* dead so she could await the promised "mysterious source" to tell her the precise location of the trove, and she could snaffle the lot? What if *that*?

The essential precondition of any creative writing worth its salt, in James's view, was "what if?" To configure the world as it might be rather than as it *was*. This was the kind of imagination James struggled to employ as a writer. Which was fine and dandy when he was scribbling the kinds of novel no respectable publisher would touch with a barge pole, but not nearly so fine and dandy when applied to daily life. That way madness lay, as James well knew, but still, he sometimes found it impossible to switch the question off, as in the case of Stephanie's treasure trove account. Was this yet another of ex-brother William's wild fabrications...or was it, just conceivably, true? That was the question. And if it *were* the latter then, given the fury she had just displayed, Stephanie might have had a motive for William's decapitation, mightn't she? In which scenario, James felt it his duty at the very least to discover whether somewhere around forty-eight Salubrious Place there lay hidden a bloodstained scimitar with Stephanie's prints on it.

"A nasty thought, indeed," James muttered to himself. "But better to leave no stone unturned."

Seven

It was the very same night while Stephanie and the brats were asleep and snoring in her bedroom—the brats' room had been vacated to accommodate James and Gabi—that James crept from beneath the sheets and went in search of the murder weapon. All over the tiny house he hunted, peering in cupboards, foraging under couch cushions, poking his nose into any crevice he could find that might house the bloody scimitar, but nothing did he discover. Not even a knife sufficiently large, sharp, or serrated to chop off a fish's head let alone that of a six-foot human like William.

Having exhausted the house, he tippy-toed out into the minuscule paved garden which sported a few wilting geraniums in pots plus a lean-to shed leaning so much it was about to fall over, and so small it could barely have contained a mower for the lawn that didn't exist anyway. It was the sort of shed an elf would have been happy to inhabit, that was about the size of it. But there were no scimitars in there either, not even one carefully wiped of blood and presumably bits of skin tissue. No scythes, no outsize secateurs, no monster scissors, *nothing* capable of the hideous crime for which he was still under the suspicion, and which he was hoping to disprove forever. Not that he would lay the blame on Stephanie should he find the murder weapon, of course. That would be too dastardly. But he *could* put it somewhere so far removed from his or his sister-in-law's environs as to render its use by *them* in the killing of William, at the very least, improbable. Possibly also tie a little note around its handle saying, "It *WoSn'T JaMeS wOt DuNniT*."

"Hrrrmph," he said, peering up at a milky full moon, the man in which returned his gaze with a supercilious smile. "Humans and their sad little lives," he appeared to be implying.

"Sod off," James told him, and was glad to see a passing cloud wipe the smirk from his face.

After that, there was nothing left for him to search so, yawning, he headed back to the house. "Headed" as if James were on some Texan ranch. In fact it only took two or three paces for him to be back in the kitchen-cum-diner-cum-family room-cum-lounge, which could only have measured a dozen square feet. The sort of space you might have expected from the latest London housing development of micro apartments based on the Japanese model of coffin hotels.

"Still, unless she's hidden it somewhere nobody will ever find it or chucked it off a cliff into the sea or something," he whispered to himself, "that pretty much lets Stephanie off the hook."

Such was his immediate conclusion, although this was his first ever sally into the art of sleuthing, and he was aware there could be other potential explanations for Stephanie's involvement in the crime. Some covert lover she'd taken to punish William for his frequent straying from marital vows by cutting his head off, although his willy might have been a more appropriate organ, even if it didn't kill him. A family member with insanity issues and an expertise in scimitar wielding she'd paid off to free the planet of William. A local art critic so enraged by William's dystopian abstract nudes he'd allowed himself to be encouraged by Stephanie to do the dirty deed as a means to ensure there would never again be another Cockburn dystopian abstract nude exhibition in St Ives. The list of potential doers went on.

It was as James was contemplating these further what-ifs while peering hopelessly around the "kitchen" that a peculiar grinding noise started up behind the ratty chintz curtain that separated off the sink and cooker.

"What the...?" he said, drawing the curtain as the grinding continued, accompanied by what sounded like footsteps in snow or mud. Squelchy.

It was only then that the horrible thought, the one that practically froze his heart, struck him. In a word: the cellar. It had never occurred to him such a tiny house might contain a cellar.

"Shit," he said as the floor beneath him began to open and someone—the "mysterious presence" Stephanie had mentioned?—said, "Hello James."

He didn't look up because he was already on his knees, hanging his head and praying for forgiveness to the God he'd so brazenly denied in all three of his failed novels.

~ * ~

"Don't be shy," said the voice as the squelchy footsteps approached, and then James felt finger-like things, possibly even flippers with toes, grip his shoulder. "Look up. You can't stay that way forever."

"Aaaagh, grrng," he said as the toed flippery things took to squeezing at his shoulder. Gently.

"You will probably not have seen a creature of my kind before, and to you, as to any human, I may appear monstrous beyond your limited comprehension, but try to expunge from your mind such value judgments. Because a person is different doesn't mean s/he is to be feared," said the voice.

"Unggrah, ung," James said, as the shoulder squeezing morphed into a kneading he was beginning to like. In some arcane way, the terror that had been rattling through his body eased, to be replaced by something resembling comfort. How this could have happened he didn't know. And didn't care. Even when he briefly wondered if he were being put under some kind of a spell, he didn't care. Maybe this was what morphine was like. Or marijuana. Or heroin. Or LSD. Never having used any of those drugs, he had no means of comparison. The kneading was nice though, consoling.

"Just a little peek?" said the voice, as the massage moved to the other shoulder and then down his spine.

And so it was that James raised his head.

If you're not a fan of the paranormal, I would perfectly understand should you set this book aside right now and watch TV instead. Not that there's much on these days apart from cookery programmes, sport, and past their sell-by-date cop shows. Should you be of the inquisitive type prepared to tolerate the idea however, this is what James saw as he turned to meet what he'd come to think of as "the phantom from cellar": an elf. The sort of being he'd imagined as living in the minuscule lean-to in the garden, tiny in the traditional way of elves, therefore, with a long beard and pointy ears. At first sight, at least. On closer inspection however, this one, who introduced him/ herself as Koleen, didn't feature *only* regular elfin masculinity, but beneath the long beard and pointy ears, also sported breasts and legs of which Marilyn Monroe would have been proud. Think androgynous sex kitten elf here. And the fingers/flippers that had been massaging James? Were flippers, hence the squelchy. S/he was wearing a diaphanous red shift.

"Kuh-kuh-Christ," said James.

"As you wish," said Koleen, morphing into a passable image of the saviour whom James—like Peter, Thomas and Judas—had so frequently denied in his three novels. One way and another, everything was getting pretty spooky.

"No, look, I didn't mean..." he said. But Koleen just smiled.

"My dear, I can be anything you want me to be," s/he said. "But always remember I have a mind of my own. Whose powers I suggest you accept without question. Meanwhile, I am at your disposal for assistance in your current dilemma. Like a bridge over troubled water, all you gotta do is call, you've got a friend," s/he added in a bizarre mishmash of Paul Simon and James Taylor songs.

Then, just like that, s/was gone in a puff of smoke, and James was left alone in his ex-brother's kitchen. Fat chance of any sleep in the remainder of *that* night, so he just paced...and paced...and paced around the bedroom, waking Gabi, who wanted to know what the hell was wrong with him all of a sudden.

"Oh, you know, things on my mind. Difficulty sleeping, that sort of thing," he said, climbing back into the bed in which Gabi had already returned to snoring. Mind you, better that than being obliged to admit to having just met a friendly bisexual elf and having his sanity interrogated in the wee small hours when it was always at its least reliable. Maybe he *had* gone temporarily bonkers what with the recent stress and everything, and tomorrow would be a brand new day. He sort of doubted it, but hope springs eternal, does it not?

~ * ~

When he eventually faced the new day, James was hoping to feel refreshed and compos mentis, but he wasn't. Instead, he was feeling brain dead, seeing as he hadn't slept a wink while Gabi continued to snore for Germany. The fear in what was left of his mind was different day, same shit. And this was confirmed when the brats Ernest and Georgina came marching into what was after all *their* bedroom to wake their guests and have games. Ernest had brought with him a toy chessboard with all the kings and pawns and stuff, and Georgina three Barbie dolls with a selection of different outfits. Resisting the temptation to tell them to get lost, James managed to remember these were children who had just lost their father in terrible circumstances, although they didn't know it yet, having been told William was away on a "business trip"—*some* business trip. Nonetheless, he nudged Gabi who stopped snoring but continued to snuffle contentedly.

"Gabi, *Gabi*," he hissed in her ear, "it's the brats."

"*Was*? (What?)," she groaned.

"The *brats*," he re-hissed, at which Ernest took offence.

"I'm not a brat," he said. "I'm a boy."

Georgina backed her brother, saying she wasn't a brat either; she was a girl.

"I got costumes for the Barbies," she added.

James girned while jabbing Gabi in the ribcage. "*Die Kinder sind gekommen* (The children are here)," he growled but with little effect apart from one bleary eye opening.

"Why are you speaking funny?" Ernest wanted to know.

"Maybe he is crazy man," said Georgina, climbing onto the bed and testing it for trampoline potential. Jumping up and down with the three Barbies clutched to her chest.

James was pretty much at the end of his rope, which was a short enough rope anyway, where children were concerned. He had never liked them or ever wanted one of his own. Far too much aggravation and with no guarantee of them growing up to be better than any other human on the planet, let alone him. Pointless, expensive, and messy was his view of procreation. No goo, goo, gooing over babes in prams for *him*, therefore.

"Gabi, *Gabi*," he was continuing to plead when Stephanie stumbled into the room in her nightie clutching a smartphone.

"It's DI Skewes for you," she said, thrusting the loathed instrument into the hand James was keeping tethered by his side in case it took to smacking Ernest and Georgina around their heads.

"Woz *he* want?" he said.

"You. At the cop shop pronto," said Stephanie. "Be nice, okay?"

"Nice to Skewes? *Nice?*"

"This time he's got a lawyer for you, so you've got no choice."

Talk about different day, same shit.

~ * ~

Contrary to expectations, however, when he arrived at St Ives PD HQ, Skewes was all sweetness, light, and apologies.

"Sorry if I upset you at all the last time we met, Doctor Cockburn," he said when they were ensconced in his little office, the 'they' to include not just him and James but also James's promised lawyer, a green-eyed redhead called Janice Peterson who winked and smirked at him when introduced.

"Only new evidence has come up, innit?" he continued. "Meaning you are now free to leave town any time you want."

Janice winked and smirked again.

"New evidence?" said James.

"Yeah."

"Pity I had to be kept in the cells for the night then."

"My client has a point," said Janice, who clearly had history with Skewes, reckoned him for a dork, and was enjoying his comeuppance.

"I was within my rights," he protested. "Twenty-four hours I can hold a person wivout no lawyers, innit?"

Janice shrugged and stared off. James was starting to like Janice.

"*Any*way, rights or no rights, what's this new evidence?" James said.

"Autopsy report on the time of death," said Skewes.

"Which was a bit late in the coming, wasn't it, Detective Inspector?" Janice rolled her eyes at her client.

"Bleedin' *system*, innit? Been telling them morgue boys and gals to get their acts together for years, bain't I?"

James watched on as the copper and the lawyer traded accusations and defences. At least it was each other they were winding up, not him.

"Anyhow," Skewes continued after some huffing and puffing. "It seems your bro bought it when you and your lady friend were already back on the train to London, so..."

"I stand not guilty as charged."

"You were never *charged*, you were only held for *ques*tioning."

Janice raised the sort of eyebrow that intimated police brutality.

"There is another small matter you might wish to communicate to my client, Horace," she said. "What one might think of as the double whammy?"

Horace—evidently Skewes's first name—nodded and shrugged. "Yeah, well..."

"The matter of the confession to the crime you received from Billy Tremayne at the same *time* you were holding my client in custody against his will."

"Hrrumph," said Horace.

Interested, James said, "Billy Tremayne?"

"Local wide boy, fisherman, and thief," Janice told him.

"Only there was no way we could *prove* it, was there? Billy's in here every five minutes confessing to things. Ask the sergeant," said Horace. "*Wants* to be banged up, does our Billy. Needs a place to sleep."

"But this time, you *did* bang him up, am I right, Detective Inspector?"

Horace nodded.

"May one ask why?"

"He reckoned he *knew* stuff, didn't he? Details. Also he had no alibi, so..."

"What stuff?" James asked

"Never you mind, Sonny. Police business that is, innit?"

It was at this point that James asked to be excused. Seeing as he was now a free man, he reckoned he was within his rights. Janice agreed. And, surprisingly, Horace did, too. Probably embarrassed by Janice's taunts in James's presence. Shaking her hand in thanks for her contribution and scowling at Skewes therefore, James took his leave.

It was as he was sauntering along the road caring little if it were Billy Tremayne or anyone else who was being accused of offing William just as long as it wasn't him, that he heard a familiar flippy-floppy squelchy sound behind him.

"What the...?" he said as Koleen in the guise of a surfer beach bum replete with wet suit and rubber flippers drew up alongside and said in an American accent, "Hi there again, James."

"*You* again?"

"I am your friend, right?"

"So you said, but..."

"No buts. Except for one. It ain't Billy Tremayne who dunnit. Meet me on the Porthmeor beach at midnight."

Then, just like that, s/he was gone.

Eight

James spent the rest of the day wandering around town with Gabi, who was delighted he'd been freed and offered to buy him lunch at any café of his choice. Ostensibly at random from their town guidebook, James chose one overlooking Porthmeor beach so he'd be able to find the way to the midnight rendezvous with Koleen about whom, in order to retain *some* reputation for sanity, he intended to tell no-one, not even Gabi. Would *you* believe a person who tells you he's recently been befriended by a metamorphic bisexual elf, and still trust him to be playing with a full deck? Probably not, especially when he's only just escaped the accusation of having topped his own brother with a scimitar and could, therefore, be considered emotionally unstable. No, no, omertà was the name of the game on the Koleen issue.

"Is not this *lovely*?" said Gabi when they found the place.

And it was. From the veranda on which they sat, there were fabulous views all along the coastline and its looming cliffs.

"Yes," said James, peering at the tapas of scorched prawns, salt and pepper squid and polenta tortilla with a side salad and a glass of white wine he'd ordered. Gabi had gone for the churros and red wine.

"I am so happy," she said. "Sad for William, Steffie and the children, but happy for you. Big relief you are not the killer, *nicht wahr?*"

He laughed, prodding a squid with his fork.

"Strange thing, life," she continued. "How long ago was it since we met in your Rose Garden, and you took me to the café?"

"Six weeks, six months..." said James, the past having become something of a blur even for one who had once boasted an eidetic Tourettes-type memory.

"And *some* weeks they have been. More like a whole lifetime. So much packed inside them."

"And now a death," he reminded her, poking at a scorched prawn to check its consistency. He'd never eaten a scorched prawn.

She nodded. "We cannot leave this place now. Not until we know who dunnit."

"Of course not."

"And we shall help Steffie and the children."

James felt less sanguine about *that* but said nothing.

"Family," she sighed with the glaze over her eyes he knew to have its origins in what she had left behind in East Berlin.

"Indeed," he said, prodding the tortilla with a finger. "Can't live with them, can't live without them."

"But at least now, we have each other." Gabi poured herself a fresh glass of red.

James took her hand and held it.

"No secrets between us." She smiled. "Everything out in the open."

"Of course." Well except for the small matter of Koleen.

"And who knows, maybe we can *help* to find out who killed William." Gabi lit one of the *Rot Händle* cigarettes she still managed to find on the Black Net and blew the pungent smoke out across the bay. "You and me, the detectives, eh, James?"

"Probably best left to the professionals. Not that there's very much professional about them."

Although, James reflected, if Koleen knew Billy Tremayne hadn't dunnit, maybe s/he also knew who *had*. Maybe s/he also knew where the treasure was. Maybe these were the secrets s/he was about to share with him on the beach at midnight. It was a tantalizing thought. On the other hand, what if Koleen didn't exist and was merely a figment of his febrile imagination, and wouldn't turn up for the meeting at all, obliging him to conclude he *had* lost his marbles? So many what ifs littered around all over the place.

After lunch, Gabi and James strolled the strand, kicking at the surf like the lovers you see in second-rate Hollywood chick flicks. All they needed to complete the scenario was a trusty hound to throw sticks for. Or maybe a message in a bottle to come floating just out of reach in the deeper water, meaning, oblivious to the ribaldry of the beach bums, they would to strip to their underwear and wade into the waves in search of it, after which, when the message told them who'd dunnit, they would celebrate their discovery with underwater sex.

In real life, however, there were no bottled messages telling them who'd killed William and allowing them to triumph over the footling investigations of dicks like Skewes. In real life, Gabi and James just got wet (and cold) feet before heading back to number forty-eight Salubrious Place to check on Stephanie and the brats. Nonetheless, he would be back on the beach at midnight for whatever Koleen had in mind as the subject of their meeting. If, of course, s/he turned up at all.

~ * ~

Which, as it turned out, s/he did. James had made his excuses to Gabi and Stephanie citing sleep disturbance similar to the night before, and the need for a dose of fresh air before he hit the hay. Braving their objections, he then made his way back to the beach, where he arrived at eleven minutes to midnight. Full moon, a few scudding clouds, night birds cawing, water sloshing about, deserted of all humans, all very romantic and/or creepy depending on how you looked at it. James went for creepy as he checked and re-checked his watch, reckoning Koleen likely to be a cum tempore sort of an elf. What to do while he waited was the question. So, like a little kid, he took to skimming flat stones on the placid sea. Well, skimming was the plan. In actuality, only one bounced more than once. The rest just sliced into the water and sank.

It was as he was working on the selection of stone number twelve that from somewhere behind him, one the size of a saucer shot across the sea, bounced thirteen times, then went into reverse gear, and boomeranged back to wherever it had come from. You will already have guessed where *that* was. Into the waiting hand of Koleen, that was where. It was bang on midnight, so forget the cum tempore business. A punctual elf, after all. Only s/he didn't look a lot like an elf, more like Marlene Dietrich in her heyday. James had to assume it *was* Koleen. Who else could it be?

"Magic makes perfect, James," s/he said gutturally before selecting another stone—one that wasn't even flat, more like a rock—and chucking it at the water where it bounced twenty-seven times before returning to its mistress.

"Rocky, rocky, in my hand," s/he then crowed in a hammy parody of Snow White's 'Mirror, mirror on the wall,' "Who's the fairest skimmer of them all?"

"You, Mistress," said the rock. "Gimme another go!"

So Koleen did and, this time, Rocky managed forty-two skims before twizzling around and returning to his/her waiting hand with a big grin on his face. James reckoned Rocky for a he.

"Oo*kay*, enough with the games. Walk with me," said Koleen, sashaying off along the wet sand and finger-hooking him to follow. "A little secret I have to tell you."

With the promise of truth on the matter of William's killing in prospect, James followed like a puppy.

"Hit me," he said when he caught up with her.

So Koleen did. Not hard but sufficient to send him sprawling in the sand.

"Bloody hell, what was *that* for?" he said, scrabbling to get back to his feet. But Koleen just giggled as s/he morphed into a Clint Eastwood lookalike.

"Teach ya a thing or two 'bout literalism," he said, firing up a cheroot with a match struck on the heel of his cowboy boot.

James was getting a bit pissed off with this performance. Who did she or he think s/he was, this Koleen?

"Stop screwing around with me," he told him/her. "I'm not some *toy*. I'm a human *being*."

"For what *that's* worth" was the rejoinder.

"You told me Billy Tremayne didn't kill my brother."

"That's right, he didn't." Clint pulled at the brim of his black Stetson till it almost covered his eyes.

"How d'you *know* that?"

It was sometime around then, as a past-its-bedtime gannet swooped on an unsuspecting cod and flew off with it in his beak, that Koleen tired of the movie star game, returned to a straight elf, albeit with Marilyn Monroe breasts and legs, and let James into her/his secret, namely that if Billy *had* dunnit, he would never have confessed in a month of Wednesdays.

"Huh?" said James.

"That's the secret of the treasure. The only person who will find it is the one who kills the last person to know its exact location, the killer then becoming the new custodian of the trove on pain of death should he or she ever admit to his or her crime. Not Billy therefore. Not if he confessed."

Unlikely to be Stephanie either, James reflected. Asking for trouble she would have been in telling him and Gabi of the treasure, let alone in the context of William's murder.

But that still begged the question of who *had* dunnit, even the intercession of some non-human treasure protector crossed James's what-if writer's mind. He put this interpretation to Koleen, but that was when s/he went coy on him.

"If only I *knew*," s/he said, batting elvish eyelashes and pulling at the elvish beard. "*Such* a mystery."

Then, just like that, she was off again. Gone in a puff of smoke.

Nine

When rookie detectives James and Gabi sat down together, the following morning, to discuss the murder, James began to reckon sleuthing wasn't nearly as tricky as it was made out to be on TV or in the movies. Already they had a motive, namely access to the secret treasure, but he instantly spotted four glaring aporias in other aspects of the case:

1) There was no viable suspect. Despite the "It wOz JaMeS wOt DuNniT" note, there was still no obvious clue to its author, and no sign of Skewes tracing him or her. Okay, so James was no longer the assumed doer, but he would dearly like to know to which *other* James the note might refer, especially as it seemed unlikely Skewes would be able to pin the blame beyond all reasonable doubt on Billy Tremayne who wasn't called James anyway.

2) How could Skewes be sure the body was William's if it had no head?

3) Where *was* the head?

4) Where was the evidence it had been chopped off with a scimitar? Also where was the scimitar?

"Hah hah," he cried triumphantly. Okay, the case was far from solved, but at least these four important issues needed resolution if they were to make any progress.

The answer to the first was particularly concerning. There must have been hundreds of Jameses wandering about St Ives on the day of the murder, Skewes's assumption it was *brother* James wot dunnit thus always having been totally arbitrary. They resolved to ask him how he jumped so immediately to *that* conclusion and, now it was defunct, suggest he run a check on all the other Jameses in town, particularly ones who cross-dressed as dystopian abstract nudes and had criminal records including GBH and/or murder.

On face value, the second objection looked slightly dodgy, even James had to admit. Stephanie had identified the body and, head or no head, surely a wife with two children would have at least a vague idea of the nature of her husband's physical dimensions, penis in particular, even if she had vomited and fainted after only two minutes of viewing the corpse. But—and this was a key line of enquiry—had there been any *further* attempts at identification? DNA testing, fingerprint analysis, blood samples and so on. And even if there had been, against what had they been measured to ID William beyond all reasonable doubt? To James's knowledge, there existed no record of any of these aspects of William's being as there had never been any prior reason to test them. No crimes, no car accidents, no hospitalization, at least not that he was aware of. Strange indeed to speculate this might have been entirely the *wrong* corpse, but worthy of examination. Okay, William hadn't been seen for some time, but maybe he'd just done a runner. What if, an awful thought but nonetheless, *he* was the killer of the headless body he'd stolen from somewhere and left as his own and was now in foreign parts living the high life, in which case there was no point in ID-ing the body *or* looking for the head. But meanwhile Skewes should bloody well *try* in case the high life in foreign parts scenario was wrong.

"What d'you think?" he asked Gabi, who was sceptical of this imaginative set of deductions but didn't show it.

"*Eine Möglichkeit*, (A possibility)," she said causing James to nod self-importantly and made a note in his shiny new detective notebook.

And thus, to the scimitar question. What was so particular to scimitar beheadings that made Skewes so certain one had been used in the murder of James's brother—always assuming it *was* his brother who had been murdered, and he hadn't buggered off to Tahiti to catch an STD like Paul Gauguin? Okay, the curved sword *had* been used for centuries in the Middle East to behead people, but what was the evidence such a weapon had been employed in this case? A peculiarly serrated Arabic blade, which had left its identifiable trademark? A so far undisclosed tweet from ISIS claiming it as one of their own? What?

"These are questions we must ask Skewes if we are to establish for once, and for all, the true nature of this vile crime," he told Gabi, who fired up a *Rot Händle* and shook her head in admiration at his deductive powers. At least, that's how he interpreted the headshake. Another reading might have suggested he was terminally unhinged, but he held his ground.

"And you'll help me out with finding the answers?" he asked her.

"With pleasure, Sherlock." She laughed.

"Thanks," said James, picking up the receiver of the old black rotary dial phone William had always refused to exchange for newer plastic models, let alone a cellular.

"Poor Stephanie without a proper phone," said Gabi, as a PC Hugo Chegwin came on the line asking 'ow he might be of hassistance and, when James told him 'ow, he was put through to Skewes whose phone rang and rang until it was finally picked up. But you know how twitchy coppers can become when faced with hitherto unthought-of questions about cases *they're* supposed to be solving. Think Lestrade in the early Holmes stories here. And Skewes was no exception to this rule. Not happy at all was he when faced with the four problem areas in the matter James wanted sorted out. Consequently, all he said when James iterated his concerns was the case was police business and police business alone, so James would be better employed combing the beach for seagull droppings or writing another of his silly stories than wasting Skewes's time with clearly barmy criticisms of his handling of the situation.

"My advice, sonny, is just piss off, and leave it to the professionals," said the DI before the line went terminally dead.

Undeterred, however, James and Gabi ignored the repeated advice to leave town, marched down to the cop shop, made their way past PC Chegwin on the outer desk in exchange for a mere ten quid, and knocked on Skewes's door only to be greeted with a flashing electronic sign on the left lintel saying: "I'm out." You may remember the same tactic having been employed by Major Major Major in *Catch 22*, the major Yossarian could only get to see when he was out.

But Gabi and James weren't buying any of that. Not only had James recently spoken to Skewes on the phone, but he and Gabi had seen him skitter into his office shortly after their arrival at the cop shop. Okay. he might have gone to the Gents or some other room meanwhile, but how would that explain the footsteps they were both able to hear by plastering their ears to his door? Unless they belonged to the cleaning lady or some interloper, but Gabi and James didn't think so, especially as the pacing seemed to be coming from right behind the door and was accompanied by the nervous cough James had identified from his last brush with Skewes.

Looking at each other interrogatively then nodding in agreement, they knocked again. Same message, this time with red exclamation marks and scowling emoticons, so they called out his name, turned the handle and pushed. Silly of him not to have *locked* the door, but that said something about his skills as a crime fighter.

"DI Skewes," said James, half expecting either a denial of his identity or the vision of a bloke's bottom disappearing through an open window of the kind employed by Major Major Major when he was on his way to being "out." But caught in flagrante delicto, albeit eyeing them malevolently, Skewes was left with no other option but to let the two amateur detectives in.

"What d'you want?" he said. "And don't give me no more of that bullshit about transy blokes called James who dress up as dustoopian nudes, or your dead bleedin' brother's body not *bein'* your dead bleedin' brother's body, or findin' his head, or skimitars not bein' skimitars. Okay?"

"Actually no, Detective Inspector. Not okay at all. We would be grateful for your perspective on all those pertinent matters. Wouldn't we, Gabi?"

"*Doch*, (Yes indeed)," said Gabi, causing Skewes to frown and eye her suspiciously.

"This woman is not English," he said. "She is *for*eign."

"Cleverly spotted, Detective Inspector. She is, as it happens, German."

"Ah hah, *German*, eh?" said Skewes, with an unsubtle mixture of distaste, disdain, and derision. Evidently thinking of World Wars One and Two and the 1966 World Cup final.

"And proud of it," said Gabi.

"Mmm," said Skewes, clearly wondering if there was anything in the rulebook forbidding Germans to speak to British police officers in the matter of British murder cases. He was sure Brexit had to have *some*thing to say about that only he didn't know what it was.

But James forestalled any such objection.

"Meet my wife and partner, Detective Inspector," he lied. "A German by birth, but now with dual nationality."

Gabi blushed and squeezed James's hand. Skewes sneered.

"Now, perhaps we could get down to business," James added, slipping across Skewes's desk the four-item agenda he had prepared specially for the occasion, the one demanding answers to his question about Jameses who liked to be dystopianly abstract naked girls, the exact nature of William's body ID given it had no head, the whereabouts of said head, and scimitars.

Skewes peered at the paper as if it were a used tampon and brushed it aside.

"I already told you this is po*lice* business!"

"Even though I am—was—William's brother."

"All our investigations are top secret. For my eyes only."

Which was, James thought, unfortunate, seeing as Skewes's eyes were...well... skewed, one looking straight forwards and the other marginally upwards.

"So you will tell us *nothing* in answer to my very obvious questions?"

This was all getting tedious as Skewes ducked and dived. Gabi too was getting restless, doubtless reminded of the Stasi's obdurate refusal ever to share information with any other East Berliner. James had to ensure she didn't explode. That could leave all sorts of shit on all sorts of fans, so he took her hand and squeezed it.

"Not a dickey bird," Skewes was saying as without forewarning the door opened and in marched a person who introduced herself as Cornish Commissioner of Police K.C. Cardynham from Truro, who waggled a finger at Skewes, and told him he'd better get his house in order pronto, and set in train the processes that would ensure these good people received the information they required or pretty soon he'd be spending his days sluicing out the station's toilets.

Skewes gawped and gasped.

So did James when he recognised the elvish eyes behind the super-copper's austere outfit and hair shaven to a crew cut. On the very tip of his tongue it was to whisper, "Koleen, what the hell are *you* doing here?" but mercifully, he checked himself with the words on the very cusp of release from his lips.

Anyway, long story short, as "Cardynham" stalked up and down the office ostensibly reporting progress—or the lack of it—to a Superintendent O'Hara at Scotland Yard on her smartphone, a chastened Skewes burbled his acknowledgement of a certain laxity in St Ives PD procedures and promised to put them right "as a matter of priority."

Behind him "Cardynham" gave James a gleeful thumbs up then bustled out of the room claiming an urgent appointment back at Truro PD HQ. Gabi and James followed her moments later, leaving a sweaty Skewes to stew in his own juice. Maybe, he would come up with some new evidence, or maybe he wouldn't. A small fictive voice in James's head even wondered what if *he* was the secret assassin and treasure hunter, which was why he was so keen to obfuscate the whole matter and bury all the traces, a local copper who'd have been bound to hear rumours around town since boyhood. But James told the voice to can it. Real life was complicated enough without him adding his second-nature what-if dimension to it.

Back on the street, Gabi told him how fortuitous and helpful Commissioner Cardynham's intervention had been.

"What a nice woman," she said. "You wonder how *she* came to hear of the case in the first place, *nicht wahr?*"

James shrugged mystifiedly.

"Let's find the local Starbucks, shall we?" he said. "I'd kill for a latte and a croque monsieur."

"And for me—*hus*band—the Americano and a croque madame," giggled Gabi.

Ten

Watching developments on the special EV (ElfVision) monitor, Koleen, whom William knew as a fully male elf called Chucklebutty, had provided for him in the treasure trove cave deep beneath the forbidding cliffs, William Cockburn chuckled. Fat chance any of *those* dimmos, including his bumbling brother and his fuckable friend, were going to be able to unpick the little puzzle he had set for them. Okay, so the secrets of the treasure and its treasur*er* were out, but with the ex-holder of that position now safely and undetectably dead, and nobody with any idea who might have killed him for the knowledge, what was to stop William from pilfering the lot? Nothing, that was what. And *what* a clever fellow he had been to come up with such an ingenious plan. Okay, so Chucklebutty had played a minor role in it—a lie because Chucklebutty had cooked up the whole bag of tricks—but who cared about some footling elf? Not William Cockburn, that was for sure. Once the diamonds and gold had been morphed into proper money and safely stored away in some untraceable offshore account, it would be goodbye elfie, and hello the limitless wealth William would use to wave two fingers at the half-arsed ignoramuses who'd scorned his art and him. To this end, he intended buying his own building on London's South Bank and stuffing it with his dystopian abstract nudes. The gallery would not be in his own name, of course, but in that of a Greek shipping tycoon and international art connoisseur Aristides Intracropolicos, whose fake website would soon be buzzing with fictive eulogies to the thus far little known work of the genius William Cockburn, thereby spawning auctions across the globe, the sales at which would make the proceeds of the St Ives treasure trove seem like peanuts and, more importantly, guarantee William's place in art history as on a par with Picasso's. And all he'd needed to do was weather the storm of vilification he'd suffered, make a few little alterations to his status, and keep his head.

Which he had both metaphorically and literally, for the head he was wearing was still *his*. That was why neither the coppers nor his pen-pushing brother would ever find it, any more than they would find his killer, seeing as he had effectively killed him*self*. Okay, so he'd had to sacrifice his body to the investigation for authenticity's sake, but that was no particular loss. Now, courtesy of Chucklebutty, he had a snazzy new one replete with a top-notch ticker, rippling pecs, quads, and a six-pack to die for—which Chucklebutty might have to if s/he spilled any beans or upset any apple carts in the process of William's future plans. Duplicitous little buggers elves could be, William had come to believe. Like women, they were fine when on your side but proper demons if scorned or thwarted. Anyway, that was the new William Cockburn for you. Same screwed-up old head, but now on a body much like that of Muhammad Ali in his prime. Talk about worlds and oysters. At least that's how William—Billy (The Kid) as he now liked to fantasize—thought of his very probably immortal future.

"Hey ho and a nonny," he trilled to himself, stroking the surface of either the Koh-I-Noor diamond or a very decent facsimile of it.

~ * ~

Above ground in St Ives, James and Gabi got married. Yes folks, after being referred to as his "wife" by James, Gabi had taken the bull by the horns and proposed.

"But it was only a slip of the tongue," James had initially protested. "Just a little lie to blindside Skewes, an empty phrase to make us seem a serious team. A joke, a..."

"Joke poke," Gabi replied. "You're the man I love, and I want you for mine. Marry me."

"Um...erm," said James, reckoning he probably loved Gabi too but still recalling the "mine, mine, mine" of the crazed episode back in King's Cross when he'd been worried about Stockholm Syndrome. Also, wasn't it the *man* who was supposed to tell the *woman* she was the one he loved and wanted for *his*? That's how it went in the movies. But maybe Berliners watched different, less gender biased, kinds of movie. After all, a lot had changed in Germany since the bad old days.

"Well, I..." he continued as Gabi grinned and took to twirling an imaginary ring around the third finger of her right hand. That was where Germans wore their wedding rings, James knew that much.

"It's just that..." he stalled as Gabi patted her stomach and looked soulful.

"Tummy ache?" he said, hoping the marriage topic had been dropped. "Rennies, those are the things for tummy upsets. Probably the croque madame you ate the other day. Too buttery I would..."

Gabi shook her head, continued to rub ever so gently, and then winked. Which further confused James. What *else* could be wrong with a person's stomach? Wind? Appendicitis? It was only when Gabi knitted her fingers, cradled her arms, swung them a little, looked down and cooed maternally that the awful truth dawned on him.

"Omigod, you don't mean...?"

"Indeed I do, *Vati* (Daddy)."

The word sounded so much like "farty" even the stunned James had to smile.

"But I thought you'd been using..."

Gabi shrugged. "Must have missed a couple," she said. "You know how it is in the heat of a passionate relationship, Jimmylein."

That's what Gabi had taken to calling James: Jimmylein.

*Any*way, what with Gabi wanting him for hers, and the prospect of a mini Cockburn on the planet, this was clearly an offer he was in no position to refuse.

"Okay then," he said.

As fate would have it, Gabi wasn't pregnant. But this was no trick she'd pulled to bag her man. What with all the excitement of recent events, she had simply missed a period or two, that was all. By the time menstruation magically reoccurred, however, it was too late. Rings had been bought and arrangements made. James was confused by the whole business, having brainwashed himself into looking forward to becoming a daddy, but he accepted the outcome with as much grace as possible, especially when a heartbroken Gabi promised they could have another go at parenthood once the murder case had been solved.

"In the end, all manner of things shall be well," she told him through her tears.

To his surprise, James found himself snuffling a bit too. At precisely what he wasn't sure, given the novelty of the experience. Self-pity was a starter, but on reflection, he reckoned it could also be the result of an emotion entirely new to him, one bordering on empathy. With Gabi's display of bravery and hope in what must have been a very dark hour for her.

"There, there," he said, taking her in a practically paternal hug. "Never mind. We'll still get married anyway."

"You are a guh-good man, Juh-Jimmylein Cockburn. To you, I wuh-will be the buh-best wuh-wife a muh-man ever had."

And so it was arrangements came to fruition, rings were exchanged, and oaths sworn. The ceremony at St Ives registry office was brief and intimate, attended by only Gabi, James, Stephanie, the brats and Koleen, who morphed into twin beach bum witnesses called Kevin and Trisha and was paid fifty pounds per twin for his/her troubles.

Afterwards, Gabi and James drove off in a hired vintage VW dormobile for a day or two in the countryside.

~ * ~

Unsurprisingly, DI Skewses's progress in the William Cockburn murder and decapitation case was proceeding at the pace of a doped snail. The only firm progress was the body having finally, and conclusively, been identified as William's by Stephanie, who had been invited back to the morgue for a more prolonged inspection and this time, without fainting or vomiting, had spotted the telltale scar on his right buttock left by the freak "Win A Goldfish" fairground accident in which he'd been shot in the bottom with an air rifle by a drunken twelve year-old not called James. Otherwise, there was little for Skewes to celebrate. Per the demands of James, Gabi, and Police Commissioner K.C.Cardynham, he had run a check on all potentially murderous cross-dressing criminals called James—as either a first or a family name—within a fifty-mile radius of St Ives and come up with a big fat zero. There were plenty of pretty nasty Jameses and Jimmies with criminal records as long as your arm on the books, but all of them for relatively minor offences for which they were currently banged up anyway. So far so bad. As was the search for conclusive evidence on the scimitar question which, given there was none, remained little more than idle speculation. And as for the missing head it had supposedly severed, a total dead end. Skewes had appointed a special team of severed head experts in his quest to find the former but, despite two weeks of rigorous dawn-to-dusk combing of the local area, they'd found nothing. And the poster campaign showing a blow-up photo of William's head in profile—snapped by Stephanie on one of their better days—accompanied by the logo IF YOU FIND THIS HEAD TELL THE POLICE IMMEDIATELY (AND DON'T TRY PLAYING FOOTBALL WITH IT!) met with a similar fate of absolute silence. What with one thing and another, Skewes was pretty well stumped, with which information James and Gabi declared themselves "disappointed" on their return from their brief honeymoon. It was all very frustrating for all those concerned, and most frustrating in particular for Koleen/Chucklebutty—henceforth to be known as KayCee unless responding to any of his/her pseudonyms—who, having been instrumental in setting up the story then handing it over to humans for a solution, was starting to despair. How *easily* they gave up, these knuckleheads! No wonder they achieved so little in their nasty, brutish and short lives.

"Holy *bugger*kins," s/he said during a brief visit to Fairyland for a little well-deserved break from the intellectual torpor of St Ives and environs. "Something I gotta *do* about this."

You will be wondering, of course you will, what KayCee's interest was in all of this. First, contributing to James's insights into who *hadn't* murdered his brother, but not telling him who had, then, master/mistress-minding the same brother's clever ruse when it came to murdering himself. A proper little trickster, I hear you opine. But to what end? I reckon nastiness of some kind would be your most likely response. After all, humans tend towards suspicion of the "other," don't they? And not just of fictitious creatures like elves, but also of other humans who aren't like them—black, brown and yellow ones if they're white, women if they're men, homos if they're hetero, Muslims if they're Christians...and all of the above also vice versa. Either way it's always the "other" guys who are bad. Ergo KayCee must have been a baddie too. Well, maybe.

I'd help you out on the KayCee question if I could, really I would, but like you right now, I just don't know the answer, so both of us will just have to wait and see. Personally, I like the mischievous, playful "trickster" idea with no clear intent at all, let alone malign one. Just an elf out for a bit of fun. But I could be wrong.

Eleven

On day nine of his cave life, William began getting bored with his treasure trove. It was all very well spending twenty-four hours a day playing with his jewels and gold ingots and dreaming of the change to his artistic fortunes such wealth could bring, but there remained the small matter of actualizing these fantasies. Not much practical future in creeping out of his hideaway daily with a few priceless gems in his hands and trying to cash them in at the local bank, however. Especially not when he was meant to be dead. However dim James, his fuckable friend, and the local bules were, it wouldn't take long until some clerk recognized the head he was still wearing, put two and two together, managed to get four, and call the cops. And, as a worldly-unwise painter of dystopian abstract nudes who knew nothing of the international gem and precious metal smuggling trade, William had no concept of any other way of capitalizing his treasure trove other than taking it piecemeal to a bank or pawnbrokers.

Also, he was running out of food, booze, and tobacco. Chucklebutty had left him with a decent supply of such essentials, but even decent supplies would run out *some* time, William knew that much. And what was he to do when they *did*? Sneak into town, stock up on life's necessities in some supermarket and, without arousing suspicion, pay at the checkout with a handful of—very possibly contraband diamonds?

Especially...when...he...was...meant...to...be...*dead.* He didn't think so. A bit of a hindrance it was becoming, this dead business. On the other hand, if he didn't eat, drink and smoke sometime soon, he would soon *be* dead. Also, his clothes were getting smelly, and there was no Stephanie knocking around to wash them for him.

"Fuck," said William, faced with the realization of the very prospect he'd so cleverly faked to his advantage was working in precisely the opposite way. How, after all, could he hope to aspire to an art history reputation even remotely resembling Picasso's if he was already dead before launching his grand scheme? No way at all, that was how much of a way.

"*Fuck*," he repeated, this time with emphasis. All in all, a pretty desirous fantasy situation was morphing rapidly into a real-life nightmare of which William had had no prior inkling. Such is the nature of hubris.

"*Ffff...uuu...ckkkk,*" he ululated into the treasure trove cave's uncaring walls a third time, but not even an echo came back. The walls couldn't give a monkey's for William's fate never mind how much— now pretty much worthless treasure—he'd fiddled the world to steal. Walls had no feelings about either humans or their treasure.

Watching in on EV during a mini-break in Fairyland, KayCee winced. Maybe now would be an opportune time for a quick return to St Ives to set a few balls rolling, balls even the knuckliest of knuckleheads couldn't overlook or misread. Funny how serendipity could work to an elf's advantage, just so long as s/he had eyes to see, that was.

~ * ~

Looking equally intently at "The case of the Cornwallian headless corpse" were the eager beaver boys and girls of the national print and TV media—as well, of course, as Jack and Jill Tweet of the Twitterverse. Why? Because they were all bored shitless with the rambling self-contradictory narratives surrounding the Brexit negotiations. Squabbling British cabinet ministers proposing some pendulum gobbledygook even they didn't understand, Brussels saying piss off to British cabinet ministers, and back and forth the debate was swinging until TT (total torpor) was starting to set in, and nobody any longer gave tuppence for who was telling the truth, or indeed if truth even came into the equation. As citizens had also observed in the U.S. of A. (Unadulterated States of Asininity) currently presided over by a megalomaniacal, misogynistic, narcissistic, septuagenarian racist with an IQ of thirty to whom "truth" had no meaning other than for its flagrant manipulation to suit his only major interest in life, i.e. himself.

It...was...all...so...repetitively...tedious and mind-numbing that even the most brain dead were looking for relief from the periphrastic contributions of hacks, bloggers and tweeters to what other hacks, bloggers and tweeters were opining about debates about debates, about reported debates, and the alternative truths and fake news spawned by them. But there had to be *some*thing left for the social and mass media to be controversial about, and what better than a headless corpse story from the depths of a county few could place on a map with any accuracy? Nothing. Unless of course, the dick brain in the White House were accidentally to obliterate China in a fit of pique, thereby triggering World War Three. *That* could be fun. But sadly for them, Dick brain shot only from the mouth, the way of most cowards, and had so far not even started a local war.

So it was that, for the want of any other way to sell their papers, hacks' speculation burgeoned as to the likely background to the murder and decapitation in Cornwall of one William Cockburn, whose name, details, and photo had been leaked by DI Skewes to a gutter press editor in exchange for a platinum Amex card. And the tweeters responded with a medley of suggestions all of their own. Overnight, William became the victim of, inter alia, not merely an ISIS sleeper cell but also: - a renegade branch of the Real IRA seizing the opportunity of stalled Brexit talks over the border between Northern Ireland and the Republic to make their pitch for one united Ireland under their control,

– A newly formed pan-national group called PVPOAE (People Very Pissed-Off About Everything) keen to make their mark in world politics by demonstrating just *how* very pissed off about everything they were by beheading people randomly, especially if found to be smiling, and thus suspected of happiness. In the photo Stephanie had snapped of William's head, he wasn't smiling at all, let alone happily, but that made no difference to PVROAE, many of whose members believed dystopian abstract nudes to be a covert symbol of contentment.

– A heavily armed transatlantic Facebook alliance of radicalized liberals seeking revenge at having been blindsided by the radicalized populists who had won the White House with their moron candidate, won the Brexit referendum with their lies, and were now making inroads into countries all across Europe. Whether William had been seen as a new breed of Cornwallian populist or had merely been in the wrong place at the wrong time was a moot point.

– The Kremlin which, emboldened by getting away scot free with the fiddling of Western elections and its Novichok poisoning programme, had upped the ante a notch and given orders for random beheadings to rattle the resolve of the already spineless West in the face of Muscovite supremacy. Whether William had been a Russian agent decapitated for leaking top-secret info to MI6, or a double-agent who'd suffered some kind of brain dysfunction, fallen between two stools and ended up being decapitated by both sides was another moot point.

And that was just for starters. In other versions, William had been offed by Colombian drug barons, the Mafia, oppressed Maoris, Martians, The Sundance Kid, a conglomerate of frustrated Internet moguls led by Steve Jobs even though he was himself already dead, plus a plethora of human/animal/vegetable rights activists with axes to grind over topics including the banning of artificial insemination of arachnids to a plague-denial campaign called BNTRTNHA (Be Nice To Rats They Never Hurt Anyone) and another called DEC (Don't Eat Carrots). Then there were the Flat Earthers. The list went on...and on...and...on...

KayCee was impressed. Never before had s/he suspected humankind capable of such wide-ranging imagination. What a shame it was that only in extremis did they evince even a fragment of the supposedly big brains that otherwise lay mainly dormant. How different from the average elf, who was constantly alive to fantasy in the most mundane of circumstances. Still s/he was grateful for their contribution, providing as it did a veritable cornucopia of angles from which s/he could set her/his Who Killed William Cockburn? balls rolling.

On the other hand, s/he reflected, how *much* more satisfying to come up with one all of his/her own, one with "elf" written all over it. Plagiarism was not KayCee's preferred modus operandi. Not by a long shot it wasn't.

~ * ~

It was two nights after his VW camper van honeymoon that James experienced the dream in which William appeared to him jabbering inchoately and making no sense at all. Dreams have that confusing way about them, don't they? One minute you're happily snuggled between the sheets and blankets doing nothing more complicated than sleeping, the next you're overtaken by rapid eye movements, and plunged into a never-never land with a cast of thousands, some of them goblins and suchlike, while the backdrop slip-slides backwards and forwards, and all over the place. Non sequiturs, deferred signifiers and metaphors abound, characters are left high and dry for no apparent reason, massive global events are crammed into picoseconds, sometimes if you get lucky you have sex, and...so...on. No wonder when you awake you've no idea what it was all about, unless you have an eidetic subconscious memory of course, which most of us do not. All you're normally left with is a profound sense of disorientation you can't shake off for hours after you awake, and a few mumbo jumbo one-liners—some of them anagrammatic or palindromic—whispered so sotto voce only fragments of them remain or have already morphed into pop songs by Elton John. No wonder Freud the fraud managed to make the international reputation for oneiric interpretations he did. Clever little plan it was of his to invent psychoanalysis as the best cure for lunacy and tell his clients it was through their dreams he could explain how bonkers they were and why. Nothing like a spot of wish fulfillment, sex and death to drive analysands even more crackers than they already were. And a nice little earner for his acolytes, especially given the "talking cures" could last whole lifetimes without anyone ever getting cured. Plenty of swanky cars and posh houses would be purchased on the back of *those* practices.

*Any*way, all James remembered of *his* fractured dream when he awoke mind-numbed in a sweat-sodden bed back at Stephanie's house at five twenty-seven a.m. on the second night of his return from the VW camper van honeymoon was a dim image of William, who'd morphed into Jabba the Hutt and the garbled line, "you will soon learn to appreciate me," which had already got distorted and turned into the Paul Simon song about all the crap he'd learnt in high school, and how it was a wonder he could think at all.

"Aaaagh," he groaned, to which Gabi responded, "*Heilige Scheiße* (holy shit)" before whacking him over the head with a pillow and turning back onto her left side to catch up with her dream about Day of the Dead celebrations in Mexico.

"Glurg," James mumbled, his head full of blurred images and unsyntactical sentences of which he could make no sense. Except that, William was somehow alive and well somewhere and wanted to tell him something. But what?

The answer to which James would have remembered if he'd had the sort of eidetic subconscious memory KayCee had mistakenly attributed to him when concocting the plan to introduce brother William to his dreams. But even elves are fallible sometimes.

"Bollocks," said KayCee when s/he realised the web s/he and William had spun had gone awry. "Have to try something else next time." The message s/he'd wanted to imprint on James's subconscious mind was not only that William was alive, well, and soon to be appreciated, but also he'd like to arrange a meet-up at a place of mutual convenience to thrash out details of the way forward. So much for the best laid plans of elves and hybrid humans. What with one thing and another, progress on the case of William Cockburn's decapitation looked like it was dead in the water.

~ * ~

Until the intervention in it of Gabi's distant cousin, unreconstructed ex-Stasi captain turned mobster Norbert Kriegskraft that was. Not that Gabi *knew* she was in any way related to the notorious villain accused but never convicted of countless robberies and a similar number of what he termed "disloyalty" assassinations. Norbert knew who Gabi was, though, because Norbert did his genealogical homework the same way he kept tabs on all the other members of his criminal *Brüderschaft* (fraternity) including, obviously, all the top-ranking police on his payroll. Erich Honecker would have been proud. Norbert also knew where Gabi was, because given the connections he still nurtured with the Kremlin—the same quid pro quo connections he used to foment populist uprisings all across Europe including the new Germany—he had access to spies everywhere.

And why, you will be asking, should this master mafioso and *agent provocateur* suddenly have taken an interest in such a minor matter as the beheading of William Cockburn, when Norbert had people beheaded all the time and thought nothing of it? Answer: in an unsigned email, he had received the account of his distant cousin's marriage to the dead man's brother in some place called St Ives, England, coupled with a persuasively argued case for William's not actually *being* dead and, furthermore, his willingness to share secret knowledge of the whereabouts of the biggest ruby ever discovered in human history for a decent price. According to the email, the ruby—sunk in the English Channel in a sixteenth century skirmish between pirates and the Mary Rose—was not only worth billions but would also guarantee its owner autocratic powers equal to those of Louis XIV or Henry VIII *and* immortality. Well, that was an offer even a gangster as experienced as Norbert couldn't refuse. Normally, he auto-deleted all anonymous emails, but not this one. Within seconds, he was hitting the keyboard asking for further details.

KayCee was pleased, and answered with a few more semi-believable lies and a load of emojis of hearts, kisses, and smiley faces. This time s/he signed the text: A Well-Wisher.

Twelve

The sudden influx of Teutons posing as beach bums and artists—Norbert's advance guard—took St Ives's regular population of beach bums and artists by surprise, particularly as the new contingent looked nothing like proper beach bums and artists.

"Who the hell *are* these guys?" was the comment heard most frequently in the bars and cafés around town in response to the posse of German speakers with army-type regulation haircuts dressed in lederhosen, panama hats, and tight-fitting black T-shirts bearing such logos as Kiss Me Kvick who kept stopping them in the streets and on the beaches asking pointed questions about some treasure trove with a big ruby in it. Norbert would have been ashamed of such amateurism, but experienced staff were hard to come by these days, and he'd had to make do with whatever riff raff he could find on the spur of the moment. Meanwhile, the locals remained puzzled.

"What I reckon is it's some sort of Kraut invasion," surmised quasi-American surfer Sandy Sanderson to ex-Sorbonne Nouveau Happening artiste Annie de la Zouche over brandies and peppermint chocolates at The Surfers' and Artists' Hideaway pub on the third night of the faux beach bum and artist invasion. Both Sandy and Annie were dressed in genuine surfer and artist outfits—cut-offs with a bare chest for Sandy and a frilly pink paint-besmirched smock for Annie, who was genuinely French.

"*Oui, sans aucun doute,*" she said before launching into a prolix disquisition on the current "*dégueulasse* (disgusting)" state of play in Brexit negotiations, and the likelihood of Germans so disenchanted with Westminster politicians' anally retentive infighting and squabbling they were preparing to take matters into their own hands. What big rubies had to do with it, Annie had no idea. Probably some sort of metonym or even metaphor, she proposed, thereby baffling her surfer buddy who had never studied anything beyond wave heights and wind strengths. Still, the evening worked out okay for Sandy, his lack of education having hurt him none. When they returned to her studio/flat, she painted him naked. Not on a canvas...on his bare body. The colours she chose were mauve for the torso, green for the arms, and yellow for the legs. Then she made French love to him, which Sandy liked a lot. It was a bit slippery, what with the oils all over him and everything, but fun. Anyway, so much for Sandy and Annie, who would soon move together to Bordeaux where they would spawn two children before divorcing and living miserably ever after.

Matters took an even more peculiar turn once the Polish mobster ZZ (Zygmunt Zbig) had been tipped off by informants in the Leibzig underworld of the reason for his sworn enemy Norbert Kriegkraft's sudden interest in the English Riviera and felt obliged to send in a few of his own low-life associates to check out the situation. And, as if that weren't enough, rival mobsters and governments from all across the European Union with advanced computer hacking technologies had also been alerted by online Polish ZZ chatter and sent in their minions to monitor an already complex situation. After all, a ruby promising world domination—that was its newly enhanced reputation—was not a prize to be overlooked in these dark days of a world overshadowed by the criminal madmen in the Kremlin and the White House. The only country missing in this scramble for glory was the UK, which was, as usual, too embroiled in internecine Brexit warfare to notice what was happening on its own shores.

So it was that the population of St Ives quadrupled practically overnight, and the "who the hell *are* these guys?" question once asked only by local beach bums and artists like Sandy and Annie became the question of choice for both Norbert's Teutonic advance guard and Zygmunt's platoon and then, in order of arrival, the first squad of goons from all across Europe about the next squad of goons. It was all very tantalizing for everybody involved, particularly DI Skewes, who had no idea what was going on. All he knew was his cells were brim full every night with one kind of a foreigner or another posing as a beach bum or artist who'd got him- or herself involved in a drunken brawl with some other drunken foreign faux beach bum or artist and badly disturbed the peace. One thing was for sure in DI Skewes's mind and that was the absolute rectitude of his pro-Brexit vote. What this country needed more than anything was NOTHING MORE TO DO WITH FOREIGNERS—a sentiment shared by KayCee, who had been happy enough with his/her work on Norbert Kriegskraft but had, yet again, not foreseen the manner in which blundering humans could screw up the efforts of even the most enterprising of elves.

"Holy *shit*," s/he grumbled as more and more of the sorts of creature s/he associated with the Mister Smiths in *The Matrix* descended on St Ives in search of the magic ruby lure s/he'd dangled for Norbert's benefit only.

Mind you, there was one upside to the current situation, namely, that within such a multitude of robotic morons, William Cockburn would be free to move around town without recognition or suspicion. And so thoroughly claustrophobic had he become in his caveful of useless baubles that William whooped with joy on receipt of the news. Quite apart from anything else, he was tiring of the whole pointless charade of international renown and was longing to get back to his easel and have sex with any dystopian abstract nude model he could find to sit for him. With any luck, he might even be able to get his old body back, but a dispirited and crotchety KayCee doubted that.

"Your bloody body's bloody *dead*," s/he re-grumbled, starting to fear the beginning of the end of whatever plans she'd had in the first place, of which s/he was already starting to lose sight. "And there's no way I can get it back," s/he added.

Which wasn't exactly true. S/he could have if she'd wanted, but frankly she couldn't be arsed. Gloomy and despondent was how KayCee was starting to feel, which was unusual for an elf and presaged the hideous fear that, because of too much contact with humans, s/he had become susceptible to their very weaknesses and might even morph into one. In the light of such angst, s/he swallowed six of her emergency ER (Elf Revival) pills—twice the recommended dose—told William he could take a flying fuck at a rolling doughnut for all s/he cared, crawled into her snuggle/pitta bed in a far corner of the treasure trove, drew across the zipper and, within seconds, was asleep and snoring.

~ * ~

James was as discombobulated as everybody else in St Ives by the recent turn of events. Everywhere he went there were Germans, Russians, Poles, Greeks, Spaniards, Portuguese, French persons, Czechs, Slovaks and Lithuanians amongst countless indecipherable other nationalities, including an improbable group of North Koreans, skulking and lurking behind every lamppost waiting to jump out pretending to be EU officials needing info on rubies and ready to pay good money for it. And that was *before* taking into account the myriads of print and TV hacks, and other news junkies from all around the world who, hearing of the bizarre events in Cornwall, had flooded the area with their laptops, smartphones, cameras, and microphones interviewing any local prepared to speak to them to discover his or her reaction to the situation. Were they anxious, breaking down nervously, hiding in their houses, considering suicide...or what? Had any of them been raped yet or attacked with nerve agents? After all, a story wasn't a story unless something bad was happening. Sadly for the hacks, though, nobody had been actually assaulted so far, although some of the locals posed happily in front of the cameras telling lie after lie about being not only raped and attacked with (Russian) nerve agents but also being hanged by their heels from telegraph poles until all the money fell out of their pockets. And so the mayhem escalated, fuelled naturally by the gazillions of opinionated texts, tweets, and blogs from all points of the globe attributing blame to all, sundry, and their mothers.

James couldn't help but think all of this had *some*thing—he didn't know what—to do with William's murder and decapitation. Or, in his worst moments of innate self-recrimination, it was the result his own presence in St Ives.

"I should never have come," he mumbled semi-coherently to his new wife at four thirty-seven a.m. of his seventeenth consecutive sleepless night. "Everywhere I go, I bring disaster. We should never have left the Rose Garden."

"Hush, *Liebchen*," Gabi whispered. "This is not *your* fault. You are not the centre of the universe, you know. There are other people on the planet, too."

"Nnnnnggg."

"Also modal verbs are a crock of *Scheiße* (shit). Should have done this, shouldn't have done that, could've done this but did *that* instead...whatever it was is already done and can't be changed, so get real. What is *is*, so stop beating yourself up."

"Grrrrundd," said James, no longer sufficiently compos mentis to compute such abstractions.

Gabi rubbed his back until he went to sleep for the ten minutes until four forty-seven, when he started the same guilt trip all over again. There were times when Gabi wondered about the wisdom of her infatuation with James Cockburn, the author, now she was quotidianly confronted with James Cockburn the man.

Thirteen

It was forty-eight hours later that DI Skewes fell off his chair and concussed himself when a person with William Cockburn's head, and someone else's body, walked into his office asking for his original body back.

"Ugh, aaagh, holy fuck, what the...?" mumbled the semi-comatose DI from his prone position on the floor while William loomed over him saying he was sorry for the intrusion. but he wanted to return to his old life and reckoned this was as good a place as any to start.

"Not too much to ask, is it? It's just I'm getting royally fed up with this body," William continued, taking off his shirt and prodding at his torso. "Nice pecs and all that, but it's just not me somehow. How would you like to go walking about the place in someone else's skin?"

At this, Skewes lost his breakfast all over himself causing William to wrinkle his nose, say "pooh!," and comment he thought coppers were made of sterner stuff.

"Probably got it in a drawer your morgue," he continued. "It'll just need a bit of a shake-up, brush down, and a transfusion, that's all. I know an elf who'll do the job. Bit of a whizz with the old metamorphics he is. We'll do a swapsie with this new one...never liked it anyway, and Bob'll be your uncle and Fanny your aunt."

Skewes farted stentoriously, prompting William to hold his nose and say pooh again. He was in the middle of commenting, "God, you really are full of shit; that's probably why your eyes are brown," when Duty Officer Grimes, sensing something amiss, marched into Skewes's office to see if everything was all right and fainted, too, once he'd connected William's head with the photofit pic of the decapitated one plastered all around the station.

"Christ…on…a…bike," said William, prodding at Grimes's splayed form with a foot. "Anybody'd think you'd seen a ghost or something. What this country needs these days is some proper coppers like the good old days."

Then, frustrated with the responses to what seemed to him a perfectly reasonable request, he took to kicking at things—wastepaper baskets and suchlike—and opening drawers full of top-secret information. He was about to feed those into a shredder conveniently placed on a side table, when into the room burst Cornish Commissioner of Police, K.C.Cardynham, who took him by the scruff of the neck, smacked him around the head a few times, threw him face down across Skewes's vacated desk and handcuffed him to a radiator pipe. For yes, folks, after a refreshing sleep—elves can sleep forty-eight hours without food or water—KayCee had awoken with a start, noticed William's absence, tracked his whereabouts on EPS (Elf Positioning System), said "shit," morphed into K.C.Cardynham, and re-materialised in a microsecond in Skewes's office.

"Bloody hell! What d'you do that for?" William complained, recognising the one he knew as Chucklebutty even behind her Commissioner of Police guise.

"Because you're a stupid twat," KayCee told him. "Now, shut your gob, and let me handle this," s/he added as Skewes and Grimes regained something resembling consciousness, staggered to their feet, clutched at each other, and took to tottering around the office on spaghetti legs. KayCee was about as impressed by their performance as William had been.

"Pull yourselves together right now, you wet nellies," s/he barked. "I've seen used Kleenex with more resilience than you."

"Buh-buh-b-but…Wuh-wuh-what a-buh-bout thuh-that thing?" chorused Skewes and Grimes, pointing with shaky—and in Skewes's case breakfast-stained—fingers at the shackled William and looking as if they might pass out again.

"Leave him to me," re-barked Cardynham. "Just a minor misunderstanding, that's all."

"Buh-buh-but, uh-uh-if that's huh-who I thuh-think it is, huh-he's meant to be duh-dead," said Skewes, struggling with the delivery of such a long sentence.

"Yuh-yeah," said Grimes, who wasn't up to delivery of any kind.

"Well, I'm not," said William, prompting KayCee to march over, smack him around the head again, and whisper in his ear, "I told you to shut the fuck up. So do it, or I'll see to it you never speak again."

"Bitch," William counter-whispered. But at least he shut the fuck up.

"Wuh-wha'd huh-he zay?" said Skewes leaning into Grimes for support, which wasn't a great plan because both of them fell over in a heap.

"He didn't say anything. I did. Something must've gone wrong with your hearing as well as your legs."

"So what did you say?" said Grimes who, despite being underneath Skewes in the heap, was recovering his wits faster than his boss.

"Hell, it's hot. Which it is in here, right?"

"And after you'd smacked him?"

"Mitch."

"Mitch?"

"If you'd done your homework like proper coppers, you'd have known William Cockburn—if that's who you think this is—had a dizygotic twin brother called Mitch. Same type of head, different body."

"Di…zyg…?" grunted Skewes, standing on Grimes's ankle as an aid to getting back on his own feet, and thereby causing Grimes to shriek, "For crissakes, boss."

"As opposed to mono," Cardynham clarified. "Plus Mitch has this big mental issue about his brother. He thinks he's him, only he isn't. Now, if you'll excuse me, I need to get him back to his asylum. Last I heard, before he escaped, he hadn't taken his meds for a week. Or at least he had, only he'd mistaken his mouth for his bottom and the results, as you can clearly see, are not great. Now, as your Commissioner of Police, I command you to look to other way while I tend to his needs."

Obediently, and also with some relief from their various pains, Skewes and Grimes did as requested, which gave KayCee/Cardynham the very window of opportunity s/he needed to pass the magic palm over William which would teleport him instantaneously back to his treasure trove cave, where s/he planned on giving him a proper bollocking.

~ * ~

Given the lack of positive, or any, feedback from their minions on the ground in St Ives, Norbert Kriegskraft and Zigmunt Zbig decided— independently of each other—to show up in town and do a little ruby research of their own. Okay, so they already headed up crime organizations with, albeit somewhat inefficient, tentacles in their own countries, but the thought of the international power ownership of such a stone would bring, could not be left to the whims of underlings. So onto planes and trains they climbed, coincidentally onto the same train from Paddington to the southwest, although in different carriages. Not that they would have spotted each other anyway, never having met in person, and only able to recognise each other through pictures they regularly massaged for fear of easy identification. Beards, no beards; moustaches, no moustaches; head hair, no head hair; nose jobs—all that type of thing. On this day, they were also sporting hats, sunglasses, and Loden overcoats with upturned collars, so detection on the St Ives station platform was a chance in a million. But chaos theory can be naughty when it comes to chances in millions.

Who could have predicted, for example that, exhausted by their journeys, both Norbert and Zigmunt would have staggered into the very same hostelry (subtly named The Buffers) across the street from the station where they would march up to the bar and order double vodkas on the rocks "shooken no stert"—neither had good English—

and then plonk themselves down on adjacent stools? Very few of us, that's who. On the law of averages, it was much more probable they'd have taken separate taxis to separate hotels and bedded down for the night. But no, here they were, next to each other, swigging down their favourite tipple. Mind you, even that situation might have passed off peacefully given the faux facial blemishes, and anti-pollution mask Norbert was wearing, and Zigmunt's adoption of a blind man's white stick, had it not been for the presence, at separate tables, in The Buffer's bar of two of their minions, one unimaginatively disguised as a beach bum, the other as an improbable artist. Neither knew each other, but both instantly spotted their leaders, having been alerted in advance to the camouflages they would be adopting for their visit.

You can guess the rest. Minion numero uno hurries up to the bar to greet Norbert by his real name, amateurishly forgetting to use the code name, "Adolf," while minion numero due repeats the error with Zigmunt (sobriquet Tanek), which causes the two hoodlum leaders quickly to down their shooken no stert vodkas, stare daggers of terrible recognition at each other, and twitch meaningfully. It was Norbert who struck first with a telling roundhouse to the head that flung Zigmunt to the floor and caused some tut-tut-tutting amongst other customers who reckoned decking a blind man to be beyond even their pales. But Zigmunt was up quickly to poke his adversary in the testicles with his blind man's stick causing Norbert to say "oooofffff," collapse forward onto the bar, and bang his head on a St Ives Best Bitter pump handle.

And then? A Wild West-style bar brawl in which none of the participants took the side of either Norbert or Zigmunt because they didn't know who they were and couldn't have given a monkey's toss, anyway. For them, this was simply a heaven-sent opportunity to be randomly violent, although of course, there were some personal scores to be settled—cuckolded husbands punching seven bells out of their ex-wives' new boyfriends, drunken poor people fisting snotty rich people for the fun of it, a cluster of genuine beach bums and artists brain-damaging a phalanx of faux ones...and so on. Pet dogs suddenly became infuriated with each other such that fur flew and yowls filled the air. Mayhem, in other words. Chairs flying about, tables overturned, bottles smashed over people's heads, bar staff scuttling for safety into lavatories and locking themselves in cubicles. Norbert and Zigmunt, both having recovered from their relatively minor injuries, and glad to be left out of the major skirmishes, edged closer to each other on their bar stools and looked on in astonishment.

"Holy shit," said Norbert in German.

"Christ on a sledge," replied Zigmunt in Polish, such that neither understood the other.

So, given this linguistic impasse, they switched to Russian as the lingua franca they'd both been taught as a second language back in their childhoods in East Berlin and Warsaw and swapped more astonished comments while shaking their heads at the bizarre state of affairs they were witnessing, in what they'd understood to be a peaceful area of the United Kingdom.

"Fucking hoodlums," said Norbert.

"Country going to the dogs," commented Zigmunt, as a pet Rottweiler called Rotty bit off the ear of a Cockapoo called Pooey.

"Probably something to do with the Brexit bollocks. Some sort of a national snafu."

"Or fubar."

"Or indeed fubar, Norbert agreed. "Look, why don't we get the hell out of here before the cops come? Not the sort of publicity we need, eh?"

"Too right," Zigmunt agreed.

But also too late because, hiding in the Gents, The Buffer's landlord George Jago had already called 999 on his mobile and been assured help was on the way, which, despite a downtown traffic snarl-up caused by an altercation between separate groups of ruby hunters, it nonetheless was. Not in the form of DI Skewes or PC Grimes—they'd been suspended from duty for brain tests following the William/Mitch incident—but a proper band of special forces types armed with tasers, batons, and dummy AK47s who marched into The Buffers, screaming, "Everybody put their hands on their heads and lie on the floor," and, once obeyed by the already knackered fighters, arresting everybody willy-nilly. Including Norbert and Zigmunt, who gave themselves up without protest. A tad humiliating for such big-time mobsters, but what other choice did they have? Shrugging at the precariousness of fate, they just climbed into the waiting paddy wagons along with all the other combatants.

Fourteen

James and Gabi's fledgling marriage wasn't on the rocks, but it wasn't going all that well either. You know how it is when two people think it will be heaven on earth to be together twenty-four/seven—which indeed the unwed James and Gabi had been for the couple of blissful months—but somehow the legal contract screws up all such romantic ideas. How the free-flowing joys of "partnership" become concretized in "marriage" and, suddenly, make you feel middle-aged, sedate, boring, and no longer on the market because that would be "adultery," which could lead to "divorce" and nasty lawyers' bills. It's the little things that start to niggle, isn't it? The wife or husband who snores on an industrial scale but won't fess up to it. The question of which one is going to do the food shopping seeing as it's no longer fun to do it together. Was it *really* such a good idea to set up a joint bank account when it becomes apparent one spouse spends more liberally than the other, causing the latter to be branded a tight-arsed meanie. Squabbles over toothpaste brands, irritations over bathroom occupation, disputes over toilet seat positioning, bickering about clothes:

"Which dress do you prefer, darling, the blue one or the pink?"

"Mmm...don't really mind."

"Go on, choose."

"I dunno." Said with shrugs and watch checking.

"*Choose.*"

More shrugging. "The pink."

"What's wrong with the *blue*?"

"Nothing."

"So why didn't you choose *it* then?"

And...so...on.

In the case of James and Gabi, such trivial bickering had been exacerbated by the former's obscure belief that all the bad things currently happening in St Ives were somehow his fault (see above), and the latter's insistence they weren't, and he was just being a solipsistic dickhead whenever he returned to this analysis, which was roughly five times daily.

"*Um Gottes Willen* (For crissake), don't you ever think about *any*body else but yourself?" Gabi would scream on each of these occasions, to which James would reply, "It's not me, it's my muse. I'm an artist, Gabi. I see deeper than the average person, who only sees what's there, and only asks why. Like Picasso, *I* see what's *not* there, and ask why not. What if it *were*?"

"Some curse *that* is."

"I thought you liked my books."

"I used to."

"That was how come you found me in Queen Mary's Gardens. I wish I was still there, and this story had never started. Life was so uncomplicated back then."

"*Your* life has *never* been uncomplicated, because you overthink it on purpose. 'Poor me because Mutti und Vati sent me away to school.' 'Poor me because William reckoned I was a dim-witted dork.' 'Poor me because my relationships never worked out.' No wonder."

"You know your problem, Gabi?"

"Tell me."

"You're cold-hearted and lack imagination. I'm going for a walk. Tell Stephanie I'll be back for dinner."

You see what I mean about marital relations being, if not terminally challenged, at least, becoming somewhat strained and, inevitably, leading to a diminution of the sex drives that had once been so exciting. "Sorry, I'm a bit tired tonight, and my hair needs washing"... and so on.

~ * ~

By contrast, although their nascent relationship was of an entirely different nature, Norbert Kriegskraft and Zigmunt Zbig were getting along rather well together. Which was sensible of them, seeing as they'd been forced to share the only remaining cell in St Ives's cop shop, once all the other brawlers had been locked up. Not much to be gained by continuing their enmity in the circumstances of being incarcerated in a twelve-foot square space with only one narrow bunk bed to take turns sleeping in, and only one stinking ConLav to pee in. So it was that a sort of *force majeure*-type pragmatism took over. Not much point in complaining when all that might mean would be getting banged up in even worse circumstances. Norbert and Zigmunt knew about those from the bad old Soviet days in both their countries, and who was to say they didn't also exist in the UK? So a burial of hatchets was the name of the game pro tem. And, unable to sleep, stripped of their mobile phones and with no radio, TV, or any other form of entertainment, the two mobsters were forced into whiling away the empty hours of the night in conversation. Yes conversation, a dying art in the early years of the twenty-first century in which the normal way to communicate with another human being—even one walking alongside you—was via Twitter. Not a question of dialogue in that case, just table-tennis monologues reminiscent of Harold Pinter plays.

But Norbert and Zigmunt transcended that. It was Zigmunt who kicked off this newly reinvented form of human verbal intercourse with the question (in Russian) to Norbert: "So what brings *you* to this pass, pal?" Notice the concern for the other rather than the self in this utterance. *Very* non-twenty-first century.

Initially, Norbert was hesitant but, remembering some of the post-Soviet Berlin freedoms of the late twentieth century, bit the bullet, and spilled beans, he'd kept bottled up since adolescence: the desolate childhood on a dilapidated housing estate, the squabbling parents, the sibling rivalry normally at fisticuffs level, the poor grades at school...

Zigmunt nodded empathetically, and said, "Ditto. Different country, same shit."

"Plus I was no good at games, especially not football."

"I was crap."

"Or making out with girls."

Zigmunt shook his head and said, "Makes two of us. Not that I was a homo or anything."

"Me neither. Just didn't have the chat-up lines, that's all. Anyway homo was against the law. The Ruskies shot you if they found *that* out. Same with you?"

"*Hanged* you for a bit, then shot you."

"So, seeing as you couldn't beat 'em, you joined 'em," Norbert concluded.

Zigmunt nodded ruefully. "The uniform was good. Gave a person power."

"Until the Ruskies got run out of town..."

"Until the Ruskies got run out of town, and our own people started beating the shit out of us for pushing them around, right?"

"Right. Ass-kissers, collaborators, Ruskie junkies, so..." said Norbert. "Like me you hit the streets, stayed there, and made it big time. Am I right?"

"Z-big time." Zigmunt laughed so hard one of their guards hammered on the door, opened the food flap, and told them to shut their faces or *he*'d do the job for them.

"Anyway, you asked me how I came to this pass?" Norbert whispered. "Sorry if I gave you too much detail."

"It's always good to talk," Zigmunt was saying when the last dim light in their cell was switched off, pitch dark descended, and through the food flap came the guard's voice again.

"Nightie, nightie, girls," it said. "Sleep tightie, and don't let the bed bugs bitie. OR I'LL COME IN THERE AND BANG YOUR HEADS AGAINST THE FUCKING WALL."

Zigmunt tossed a zloty coin hidden in his shoe but Norbert won, so he got the smelly cot while the Polish gang master curled up on the floor. But both were smiling.

~ * ~

Monitoring the development of this unexpected relationship on ElfVision, and then comparing it with James's and Gabi's, KayCee shook his/her ancient head in continuing perplexity at the human pusillanimity she'd noted across how many centuries now—ten, fifteen? S/he'd lost count. How the animals with the biggest brains could screw up even the most felicitous of circumstances, yet blossom in the worst. There had to be something faulty with their wiring, s/he had come to reckon, the same wiring that enabled them to believe they'd been created in the image of the supernatural beings KayCee knew for sure not to exist, gods who were deemed capable of guaranteeing afterlives of either eternal bliss or eternal misery depending how well or badly humans had behaved while in their zone.

"Such bollocks, just one more 'what *if*?' turned into a truth," s/he muttered to herself during an ElfVision mini break for adverts—higher quality sylvan wings, training opportunities for novice elves, that sort of thing. "They can't even agree on what 'good' and 'bad' *are*. Like, killing is bad if you're a 'murderer,' but okay if you're a soldier. Also, it's good to kill animals so you can eat them because some god said so. No wonder they fuck up so often. Faulty wiring..." s/he was musing as ElfVision switched focus to a Developing News story showing a crazed person dancing naked on the roof of St Ives art gallery.

"Oh, William, for fuck's *sake*," said KayCee morphing rapidly into Commissioner of Police K.C. Cardynham and teleporting him/herself to the scene.

~ * ~

Having dragged him back to the cave from Skewes's office in her Cardynham guise, KayCee had given William the bollocking of his life, telling him if he ever dared escape again, she'd have his minced balls on toast for breakfast, lunch and dinner and then transmute him into a toad.

"See how you like *that*," she'd emphasized, to which William had shrugged, girned, and claimed it was his God-given right as a human being to do what the hell he liked, and she could go take a flying fuck at a rolling doughnut. So KayCee had shackled him to one of the iron rings s/he'd installed in a dank cave wall and said, "Get out of *that* if you can," before turning her/his attention to more important matters.

Yet, in a way that beggared belief, somehow William must have because, as she joined the throng of rubberneckers, real and faux artists and beach bums, and police persons, there he was prancing about stark naked waving a banner bearing the message: FREEDOM FOR DYSTOPIAN ABSTRACT NUDES—into one of which he had apparently turned himself. Daubed in variegated hues of purple, red, and yellow he was dancing the Twist to Chubby Checker's "Let's Twist Again" on a hastily rigged sound system, while miming masturbation with a foot-long green dildo.

"Bloody *hell*," commented a number of rubberneckers as K.C.Cardynham elbowed his/her way through them to the front of the mob where s/he yelled, "Get down from there, you daft twat, or I'll come up there and make you!" at which William momentarily stopped twisting, peered down, focused and counter-yelled, "You and whose army, Chucklebutty?" through the strains of Chubby asking people if they remembered when things were really hummin'.

"Nice try, Commissioner," said the copper standing next to him/her, PC Peter Pawley, who had a special police "psychodynamic" diploma in TNDFR (Talking Nutters Down From Roofs), "but leave this to the expert, okay?"

"Hrrrmmmphh," said KayCee/Cardynham, shrugging but zipping her/his lip.

"Ookay then, so watch, listen, and learn," said Pawley, placing against his mouth a special psychodynamic megaphone through which he took to whispering amplified persuasive messages about loving mothers, furry animals, Chopin concertos, calming Mister Morphine tablets, chocolate wrapped liquorice sticks, expert whores, and a host of other goodies William could expect if he were to be a good boy, give himself up, and come down quietly.

"Nobody's going to hurt you if you just do me this one small favour," added Pawley when his list of temptations was over. "One small step for you, but a huge step for…"

"FUCK…THE…*FUCK*…OFF, FUCKWIT, THIS IS A *HAPPENING*," was William's reply while ejaculating cleverly aimed faux sperm (rice pudding) all over Pawley's upturned face, causing the officer to clench his fists, splutter, and be replaced by PC Dennis Dickery, who took aim with his rubber-bullet-loaded AK47 and told William to get his arse off that fucking roof right now, or he was a fucking dead man.

The ante was being upped, no question. But William just rewound Chubby to verse one of "Let's Twist Again," fiddled with his dildo, and screamed down, "I DOUBLE DOG DARE YOU, SHIT-FOR-BRAINS."

So, never one to duck a challenge, Dickery loosed off two rounds, neither of which hit its target as William danced, weaved, sang "Dystopian Abstract Nudes for*ever*," in a very rough approximation to John Lennon's "Strawberry Fields for*ever*," took off his foot-long green dildo, flung it down into the crowd much in the manner of a footballer tossing his shirt after he's scored a winning goal, and leapt into the air.

It was just as well PCs Pawley and Dickery, plus their back-up ambulance team, had come equipped with emergency landing gear in the shape of a super-soft-yet-hyper-reinforced trampoline guaranteed to save jumpers leaping from heights of up to a thousand feet, otherwise William would have been a dead man, that was for sure. As it was, after he magically landed in the very spot to which KayCee had guided his flailing body, he just bounced up and down a few times then lay motionless, exhausted but still chanting the praises of dystopian abstract nudes. Which was a victory of sorts, because there's nothing the media like more than a freak story, and William's was perfect, thus granting him the very oxygen of publicity he'd craved when planning the spectacle in the first place.

Before all that, however, KayCee whisked him away back to their cave where s/he planned on shackling him to its walls with even thicker chains and guaranteed unpickable Yale locks.

Fifteen

Norbert Kriegskraft and Zigmunt Zbig were released from incarceration without charge the following morning for the reasons that:

1) Coppers even dimmer than Skewes and Grimes—who remained on gardening leave for further mental tests—had joined up no dots and so remained unaware they had two mega-mobsters in custody,

2) The cop shop needed cells in much the same way as NHS hospitals needed beds, causing doctors to recommend for early discharge patients barely able to walk or remember their names.

Freedom was a great feeling for Norbert and Zigmunt who were now blood brothers having scratched palms and swapped the red stuff Native North American-style in the wee small hours. In this axial ceremony, the pair had also resolved no longer to squabble but to pool their resources, and not—as you might have expected— to create a German/Polish super-crime empire but instead, in order to compensate for some of the havoc they'd wreaked in their lives so far, to work together on a project named HAH (Harmony Among Humans).

The first step towards achieving this noble goal was to instruct their faux artist and beach bum troops that the whole "world-power ruby" story was just a fantasy, so they should stop beating seven bells out of each other searching for it. The second step was jointly to contact the leaders of all the other countries sponsoring "the ruby quest" and persuade them to call off their sniffer dogs, too. And you know what? Within a mere two days, the plan worked, and peace broke out in St Ives, causing widespread amazement amongst locals who had become accustomed to regular affray in their taverns and on their streets.

"Blimey, dunno what's happened, but I like it," said Vinny Vingoe to Harry Arscott over peaceful pints of Cornish Best bitter in the equally fight-free downtown hostelry, The Mule and Parrot.

Harry liked it too, although he didn't know what had happened either.

"Bleedin' funny," he replied. "Like magic."

Which was a sentiment echoed across town, although there were, of course, exceptions to it, particularly amongst the criminal fraternity many of whom had prospered while police concentration was focused on gang warfare. "Bollocks, just when things were going so well," was their common refrain. Ditto the small army of impecunious local artists who'd taken to pimping for their WAGs (wives and girlfriends) while the coppers were looking the other way.

And then there was Sir Monty Mulberry, the constituency's Tory MP, who'd been happily embezzling the government funds sent from Westminster to crank up the violence to endemic proportions in order to distract national public attention from the quotidian Brexit cock-ups only to find the money tap suddenly turned off.

"Bugger me with a broomstick," said Sir Monty to his fourth trophy wife Martina. "Just when things were going so well. Now, I'll have to sell the country cottage, the Rolls, the bally yacht, and..."

"And think of all the dosh you'll have to fork out when I take you to the cleaners for the divorce," said Martina, who was thirty-six years younger than Sir Monty and had only married him for his money, and a—never materialised—modeling career. "Bysie, bysie, Sweetie Pie, have a nice life," she'd added, marching out of the seventeen bedroom mansion perched on the edge of the very cliff of local treasure trove mythology off which Sir Monty would soon be leaping to his demise.

Mind you, Tory Party HQ was happy enough with that once the media boys and girls had concluded the suicide was inspired by Sir Monty's rabid antipathy to the latest piece of swivel-eyed, back-of-an-envelope horseshit the PM had concocted to both stay in the EU and leave it at the same time. Lesser men had merely cavilled pathetically in both houses of parliament, but at least Sir Monty had had the cojones to put his life on the line.

"Good old Monty, eh?" said Lord Simon "Squiffy" Snodgrass to Sir Anthony "Action Man" Auguebleak over tea and crumpets at The Athenaeum Club in Pall Mall. "Solid to the end, eh? Doing the job he was paid for to the *bitter* end."

"Indeed, Squiffy. One feels a special club plaque might be in order, does one not? To impress on future generations the vital importance of true Britishness in face of the European menace."

"I shall propose it to the Inner Council, Augers. No better memorial could there be to a Tory of such Churchillian dimensions."

Such was the ambience in which the Tory Party as a whole was guiding the nation to the edge of a metaphorical cliff similar to the actual one Sir Monty had jumped off. It was called a "No Deal" Brexit, which Downing Street was busy assuring the population would be wonderful for jobs, international relations, and trade with thriving economies such as those of Vietnam and The Falkland Islands. Better by far this would be than to sacrifice to the "Beasts of Brussels" Britain's sovereign right to remind itself that once (a long time ago), it had an empire on which the sun never set, and the God-given right to treat all foreigners as inferior races, and thus, deport them from its shores whenever it felt like it.

Which wasn't a view universally accepted or applauded, of course. No siree. There were plenty of protesters' voices to be heard. Vide the "FOLLOW ME, YOU LEMMINGS, AND ALL WILL BE WELL," cartoon caption in *The Daily Snitch*, for example, above a picture of hordes of raggedy-trousered, pasty-faced patriots marching behind Union-Jack-waving Prime Minister, Fanny Fortenbra, as she teetered on the brink of the White Cliffs of Dover ready to leap into thin air and an unknown splashdown in The English (not French) Channel.

Anyway, so much for politics. What of Norbert Kriegskraft and Zigmunt Zbig?

~ * ~

Well, of Zigmunt, there is no further information except that he left St Ives for an undisclosed destination at which he may or may not have arrived, given nobody knew where he was going in the first place. All that can be said for sure about him is that his name was suddenly removed—along with Norbert's—from Europe's Most Wanted Mega-Mobster list. For all we know, he may have become a Christian or a Buddhist or whatever.

As for Norbert, he *did* stay in St Ives, not only to continue promoting the interests of HAH, but also to track down his distant relative, Gabi, of whose whereabouts, you will remember, he was cognizant. And as serendipity would have it, this meeting required very little research and was ultimately achieved entirely by chance at the St Ives downtown Starbucks where Gabi and James were sharing lattes and *croque monsieurs* and *madames*. Just one look across the crowded room and, checking the photo he carried with him, Norbert spotted her, marched over, and avoiding any beating around bushes, introduced himself in practically Alcoholics Anonymous style.

(NB. The dialogic aspects of the following section were originally conducted exclusively in German but for ease of reading they have here been translated as best as possible into English.)

"Hi there, Gabi, I'm Norbert, and I'm a recovering ex-Stasi officer and big time mobster. I'm also your long lost cousin several times removed."

Unsurprisingly, both of them goggle-eyed, Gabi and James stopped munching on their *croques* and spilled their lattes. It wasn't that Norbert *looked* frightening in his cut-off blue Levis and red LOVE LASTS T-shirt, but the news he was not only an ex-Stasi officer and gangster but also related to Gabi was pretty gobsmacking.

"Um...erm...oh...well...um...gosh...um...pleasetameetcha," said Gabi, while James lay a husbandly hand over her arm, eyeballed Norbert as fiercely as he was able—which wasn't *very* fiercely—and asked for ID.

For which Norbert, like a good boy scout, had come prepared. Unfazed, he produced from his satchel his ancient Stasi membership card replete with his name and a photo of him in full uniform, *and* a copy of the Wanted Dead or Alive poster with his picture that had once graced all the Berlin *U-Bahn* stations.

"And you're saying that's *you*?" said James, who had become as alert as any of us to telephone and computer scammers and was wondering if the practice had been extended to face-to-face encounters.

"The *old* me," Norbert confessed. "I'm younger than that now. Would you like to see another pic?"

"Shuh-shuh-show us," Gabi managed to gurgle.

Which was when Norbert took from his satchel the HAH publicity advert he'd attached to lampposts all around St Ives.

"This is the new me," he said. "But, before you believe me, I recommend you compare *very* closely these pictures. Many times, to evade the law, I have had work on my face but never on the eyes or ears. Check the ears first. One is, and always has been, two centimetres higher than the other. Nothing could change that. Nor the eyes. One looks straight ahead, the other a little sideways. Check the photos, then look at me. I now have different hair, thicker and a new colour, and different cheeks, do I not? Different..."

"Hold it right there," said Gabi, distant recognition suddenly dawning. "You know who you remind me of?"

"No," said Norbert.

"My little brother, Klaus. He, too, has one ear higher than the other, and one eye looking a little sideways. At least he did the last time I saw him, which was back before I did the runner to the West."

Norbert nodded sympathetically, then, after relaxing sufficiently to ask a passing waitress for a *doppio espresso*, ventured the view the similarity might well be of genetic origin.

"Also, I know this Klaus of whom you speak," he added. "No sinner like me, instead a fine young man."

James removed the hand from his wife's arm as her eyes widened, and she asked Norbert for details of her long-lost sibling.

"Once a shit-hot footballer for Dortmund in the *Bundesliga*," said Norbert. "But last I heard, now he is coach of a big team in this country. Tran-something. Tran*more*?"

Knowing nothing of the game that obsessed millions, Gabi and James looked on and smiled obliquely as Norbert hunted his memory banks for the accurate name of Klaus's new team.

"Tran*meer*," he tentatively came up with. "Tranmeer Roofers?"

James frowned. Even *he* knew there were no "roofers" in the football league. There were "uniteds," "towns," "cities," "wanderers," "athletics," aplenty, but no roofers. In a blistering moment of mnemonic concatenation, however, he had it.

"Tranmere Rovers," he said triumphantly.

"This is *it*," said Norbert. "Very big team, no? Nearly as big as Liverpool."

James didn't think so, nor did he know where Tranmere was, but to keep Gabi happy, he nodded enthusiastically.

"Wow," said Gabi, who was beginning to like this several times removed cousin, despite his background. The Stasi part she repressed in memory of her brainwashed childhood, but the gangster bit she quite warmed to. Gangsters were *so* romantic in the movies. Also, if he could somehow put her in touch with Klausie, that could be fun, too. And maybe, with his intimate knowledge of police and criminal procedures, this Norbert might be able to help out with the peculiar matter of the apparently undead William who, after his naked antics and arrest by the person identified in the media as the Cornish Commissioner of Police, had, yet again, vanished into thin air.

So it was, after the trio had decamped to a hostelry named The Flea and Ferret for more potent libations, that she told Norbert the whole story so far and, always one to enjoy a good mystery, he gladly agreed to stick around and help if he could. At which Gabi hugged and kissed him, which James didn't like all that much, but then family *was* family, however newly discovered.

Sixteen

Stephanie wasn't missing William all that much, especially not on the occasion she drank a whole bottle of vodka and, while James and Gabi bratsat Ernest and Georgina, attended a local Sixties' revival beach party where she hooked up with Roman faux artist Arturo. Arturo was sooo un-William, sooo Italianately suave and self-assured with his fine tan and the jet-black hair to his shoulders with a fashionable knot on the crown. Into the wee small hours under the moonlight they twisted, shimmied, loco-motioned, walked the dog, and waltzed/dry-screwed to the rousing sounds of The Beatles, The Stones, The Animals, The Kinks, The Who, Cream, and, of course, The Beach Boys. Arturo's English accent when he whispered lines from "God Only Knows" in her ear drove her nearly crazy. It was even *more* knicker-wetting when he whispered in Italian, never mind, she didn't understand a word. For a woman with two small children and a newly undead and soon-to-be ex-husband, this was magic indeed, especially when the revivified William—from what she'd seen on the extensive TV and social media coverage of his recent naked rooftop antics—was not only clearly batshit but had, from somewhere, acquired an entirely new body. "No, no, give me Arturo any day of the week," was Stephanie's idea. Also, in their after-party sand-dune dalliance, she reckoned his thingie was at least two inches longer than William's and, possibly, a centimetre or two thicker. No wonder when, postcoitally, Arturo asked her if she'd ever heard of buried treasure around these parts at all, she admitted to some knowledge.

"Do what you just did all over again, and I'll tell you," she moaned flicking bits of sand from her nipples.

So Arturo did and, when he was done, Stephanie moaned, "Prob'ly jus' some silly story."

"I do not care 'ow silly, *tesoro mio* (darling)," murmured Arturo nibbling an earlobe. "*Any* story you tell I will keep in my 'eart forever," he added, nuzzling a newly sand-freed nipple.

"Oh, oh, Arturo," said Stephanie. "Kiss me."

So, obligingly, Arturo did. Frankly, he was getting a little tired of bonking then schmoozing this silly bitch, but hidden rubies were hidden rubies and business was business.

"Ah, aaahhh, such lips. I could kiss them all of the night," he said when the kissing was over. It was a line he'd used maybe a thousand times before during his Casanova-ish career but, never having experienced such compliments from William, Stephanie could happily have gone on listening all of the night. With which desire in mind, she requested Arturo to kiss some other parts of her he might find equally tasty.

"*Ma che cazzo* (Oh, for fuck's sake)," muttered Arturo under his breath, but nonetheless dutifully muff dived so expertly as to cause Stephanie to arch her back and writhe with such drama, he feared she might have a seizure, and then be unable to tell him anything of the hidden ruby.

"Aaaaaaah, ooooohhh, aaaaaaah," she continued to ululate. So loudly, Arturo began to worry her wails of passion might be mistaken for SOS wails of anguish. And there was nothing he needed less than for other renegade faux artists and beach bums like him—those who'd paid only lip service to Norbert's HAH—to come running to her rescue and steal her treasure trove secret from under his very nose/dick.

"*Stai zitta* (Shut the fuck *up*)," he therefore said, clamping a hand over her mouth and replacing the lips over her groin with a knee while peering hither and thither for signs of incoming saviours/rivals.

It was renegade HAH signatory and giant faux beach bum Benji from Belgium who came to Stephanie's aid crying, "Rape, *rape!*" before hoisting Arturo up by his jet black locks with one hand and, with the free one, kneeing him so hard in the balls that Arturo doubled over like a deflated lilo, said "oooooooommmmpphhh" and lay still.

That left Stephanie looking pretty well up shit creek without a paddle, especially when Benji took to leering at her nakedness, licking his lips, and unbuttoning his cut-off Levi's.

"No, *no*, please no," she shrieked at a smirking man in the moon as Miguel from Madrid, Jean-Paul from Paris and Arno from Amsterdam joined the party, all three of them also leering, licking their lips and freeing their manhoods from their pants. The situation had gang-bang written all over it…until William appeared out of nowhere, that was. Within seconds, he flattened all four would-be rapists with a series of taekwondo Twi-meo Yeop Chagis (flying side-kicks) before jumping up and down on their exposed genitalia, grabbing Stephanie from the sand and, with her hanging from his neck, running even faster than Usain Bolt back to the safety of his cave. It was all very dramatic.

"*William*?" I hear you say. "I thought KayCee had shackled him so firmly, he would never escape again."

Well, s/he had. But hearing and seeing Stephanie's distress out on the moonlit beach, s/he had offered him this one last chance at redemption, given him superhero powers, and set him loose.

And how grateful Stephanie was to her newly undead, and she'd hoped soon to be ex-husband as he sped across the sand, swam across an inlet with her on his back and, on reaching the mouth of the cave, dragged her inside, placed her on a special inner-cliff trolley and wheeled her along a dank and dripping tunnel until they reached the sconced candlelit sanctum where KayCee was waiting with a change of clothes, cups of tea and a packet of Hobnob biscuits.

"Nice work, Willie," s/he said.

"Willie" was what she called William on the few occasions he had behaved himself while in his/her custody. More often—particularly after the naked dystopian abstract nudes fiasco—she called him "Fuckwit."

"It was nothing," said William, shrugging and dismissing his heroism much in the manner of Tom Cruise after saving the planet, yet again.

"*William*, oh, *William*," was all a pale and distraught Stephanie managed to utter before falling into a dead faint, and having to be laid out on a palliasse, and covered with a bespoke, pink, fairy blanket that guaranteed twenty-four hours of unbroken sleep, and the sorts of dreams a three-year-old would be happy with.

There remained the question of the adulterous act with Arturo in which she'd been caught *in flagrante delicto*, but Stephanie would worry about that another day...month...year...lifetime. It was her soon-to-be ex-, newly undead husband who'd saved her after all, sooo...

So out the lights all went and, within femtoseconds, Stephanie was snoring for England.

~ * ~

After twenty-fours of bratsitting and still no mother back home, Gabi didn't take kindly to James quoting Oscar Wilde's famed epigram, "To lose one parent may be regarded as a misfortune; to lose both looks like carelessness."

"Do not be such a *hochnäsiger Schwanz* (snot-nosed prick)," she told him. And with some justification, seeing as it was she who'd done ninety-nine percent of the bratsitting, while James claimed to be preoccupied with notes for a new novel about loser-in-love Jocelyn Joynson who, reduced to desperation after a whole lifetime of losing love, including the non-existent adoration of his absentee parents, was on the cusp of resolving to decapitate his latest squeeze, Miranda O'Keefe, unless she abandoned all other interests in life apart from him. In the latest chapter, Jocelyn has Miranda shackled to an iron bedstead with in one hand a crinkly brown parchment awaiting her signature to this contract and, in the other hand, a quill pen dripping red ink that looks a lot like blood. Jocelyn stands alongside her, toting a finely honed silver scimitar and saying, "Sign on the dotted line or lose your head." Since William's beheading—and despite his brother's re-appearance with the same head but a different body—James had become pretty heavily obsessed with decapitation.

Anyway, that was James's excuse for not playing any games at all with Ernest and Georgina or reading them bedtime stories while their mother was out getting romanced by Arturo and saved by William or, during the following day when she didn't return home, playing computer games with them, or indeed even recognizing their existence.

"Sorry, I'm a writer," he told them. "More important things to do."

At which, Gabi was on the cusp of telling him he was a self-indulgent prick with a poker up his arse with whom she would *never* bear offspring but restrained herself in order not further to disturb Ernest and Georgina who were already beginning to ask when Mummy was coming home.

"Soon, soon. Any minute," she told them into the deafening silence of Stephanie's non-arrival. In such circs, her frustration at the Oscar Wilde quote was understandable, especially when eleven year-old earnest Ernest decided he wanted to know what it meant.

"Nussink, *nussink*," she told him, her generally speaking decent English accent slipping in her consternation. "Just some rubbish. Go back to your Minecraft."

But Ernest was tiring of Minecraft as a little kids' game and pining for the upgrade to the Grand Theft Auto V Stephanie had consistently denied him.

"Shan't," he therefore said, at which Gabi was sorely tempted to clip him around the ear and was only restrained from so doing by James—despite Miranda O'Keefe's parlous position—overhearing, intervening, and saying if the child was interested in literary figures and clever word play, it was his right to be informed.

Gabi withdrew the hand held ready to clip Ernest around the ear, and eyed James warily. "Okay, all right," she eventually conceded. "Only keep it simple, okay? The kid is only eleven."

"Nearly twelve," Ernest protested. "Almost a teenager."

Which cut no ice with James where simplicity was concerned. You know how it is with university teachers, even ex-ones like James, how they adore the sound of their own voices and crave an audience, *any* audience. So it was that he launched into a fifteen-minute history of Edwardian England, followed by a ten-minute explanation of Oscar Wilde's role in it—including his jailing for homosexuality—all of this topped off by a twenty-minute exegesis of linguistic tropes with particular emphasis on *double entendres.* By the time he'd finished, Ernest had passed through the glassy-eyed catatonic stage several times and, on the verge of narcolepsy, collapsed to his knees as if in prayer.

"So you see, laddie, when Oscar uses the verb "to lose" in his witty remark about parents, he is employing it simultaneously in two quite different contexts, as if losing a parent were of as little importance as losing a train ticket, hence the humour some might even term irony. Are...you...still...listening, child?" he was saying on the verge of clipping Ernest around the ear exactly as Gabi had intended in the first place when into the room burst William, who swept both Ernest and Georgina into his superhero-type arms and cried, "You're safe now, children. Daddy's *ho-oooome.*"

Well, you can imagine Gabi's and James's horror as they fled into each other's arms at the apparition of the freak they'd last seen dancing naked demanding recognition for dystopian abstract nude before leaping off a roof onto a trampoline, and then being arrested by the Cornish Commissioner of Police and, hopefully, banged up for the foreseeable future.

"Wuh-wuh-*Will*iam?" James dared ask.

"The same, little bro. Put the kettle on, would you?"

Seventeen

Faux artists and beach bums Arturo, Benji, Miguel, Jean-Paul, and Arno were not the only ones to go on believing in the authenticity of the "magic ruby" narrative Norbert had tried so hard to bury with the HAH initiative he'd established with Zigmunt Zbig. There were plenty of others of their ilk still lurking around St Ives. Okay, they were no longer publicly street brawling, but that didn't mean they'd all quietly gone home to their respective countries. Why? Because their bosses in those countries didn't believe Norbert's narrative either, many of them dismissing it as hooey or fake news, so Norbert and Zigmunt could clear the ground for their *own* pursuance of the very prize that would allow *them* to create the greatest criminal empire in human history. So the faux artists and beach bums continued to skulk about St Ives, albeit with a much lower profile. Some even married St Ivian girls to consolidate their respectability in the town.

And so things might have continued in this low-key way until the biggest fraudster of them all, American president—or CEO of USA Inc. as he preferred—Dougal Klank joined the party with a lust that began to disturb the equilibrium of even Kremlin supremo Igor Ripurpantzov. Until recently, Igor believed he had Klank in his pocket, having masterminded his election as president/CEO, but now the *pridurok* ("dork" in Russian) appeared to have lost the few marbles he'd ever possessed. Under the threat of more court cases than he could count—for sexual harassment, business malpractice, nepotism, xenophobia, treason, and general badness, all of which were edging him ever closer to impeachment—he appeared to be speaking *entirely* through his arsehole. When he *spoke* at all that was, seeing as his preferred means of communication was tweeting ungrammatically from his toilet seat at six a.m. And now that Igor had found out from the deepest of his deep throats in Washington the *pridurok* had expressed an interest in acquiring the ruby, "as a last-ditch effort to save his ass from getting kicked from here to hell," he was worried. There could be only one planetary controller, and that was Russian President For Life Igor Ripurpantzov, hence *his* resolve to find the ruby before Klank got anywhere near it.

And Igor's deep throat was dead right about Klank's ruby desires. Up to his eyes in so much shit they'd turned brown, as a number of Washington wits had commented, he spent no time at *all* governing America by comparison with the five percent of it he'd once sacrificed to the job—the other ninety-five percent being devoted to golf, philandering and self-adulation. These days, however, with an approval rating plummeting by the hour, he spent every waking moment firing off tweets rubbishing all the press except Fox as "enemies of the people," the women he'd molested or raped as "lying whores," the Democratic party as "Commoonists [sic]), dark-skinned immigrants as "brown-nosing thieves, 'rapers,' [sic] and 'terr'ists,' Republicans who didn't support him as "cowards and traitors," all the people he'd fired from the White House and gone on to publish uncomplimentary books about him as "liars," "scumm" [sic], and "losers"...the list went on and on and on...and *on*. Klank had been like this since babyhood. Those who refused to chuck his cheeks and tell him he was the prettiest and smartest guy in the room he "stiffed." Trouble was, the plan wasn't working any more. Guys and gals were stiffing him right back and not just in America. In a recent poll of the world's nastiest leaders, he'd come top. Only in those countries whose acquiescence he'd bought with (probably fake) dollars was he hypocritically courted. And now the truth about Dougal Klank—that he *was* the trumped-up *pridurok* Ripurpantzov had always known him to be—had become universally recognized, he'd been forced onto the defensive. After all, there's nothing a dyed-in-the-wool narcissist can bear less than opprobrium, hence the obsessive interest in the St Ives magic ruby.

"You gotta get it for me," he told Lester Pferd, his fourth chief of staff in as many months, all previous holders of the post having been fired for either leaking to the "enemies of the people" such comments as "the guy's a fucking moron," or not carrying out their orders to tell Fox and Friends Dougal was "the finest president/CEO America had ever had," including in their statements specific reference to his nice hair, prowess at golf, and enormous willy. Such were the attributes Klank reckoned to be the prime reasons for his election to the White House he was in the process of renaming Klank Towers and had already opened to the public at the cost a mere million dollars a ticket. Not, unsurprisingly, that very many visitors had taken up this wonderful offer, although Klank claimed them already to be in their hundreds of thousands. "And worth every last dime," he'd opined in one of his mega-advertising tweets before going on to describe the glories of rooms crammed entirely with pictures of himself in various garbs, including one of him dressed in the kind of toga he reckoned Julius Caesar to have sported.

"Whut?" said Lester, the pair sitting the ex-Oval Office newly renamed the Round Office, seeing as it was decked out with miniature faux fairways and putting greens.

"The magic *ruby*," Dougal spat through a mouthful of burger and Coca Cola.

"Ookay, *that* one. The one you keep bustin' your balls over."

"The one in Corkville, Brit'ny," Dougal confirmed.

If you'd placed Klank in front of a map of Europe, he'd have had difficulty locating England, let alone London. As for Cornwall, not to mention St Ives, well...

"The one that can make me king of the whole world. Get right on it, you wanna stay in a job."

Pferd eyed his new boss, chewed on his burger. and washed it down with a hefty swig of cola. "That old story again?" he said.

"The same. And you git on it, bozo, or you are yesterday's fake nooz. Now, git the hell outta my office. I got a plane to catch."

Dougal Klank only travelled anywhere on KlankForce One and circled around safely in the air until the very last moment before being guaranteed a thoroughly researched "no danger" touchdown with a waiting bulletproof limo into a town guaranteed to be packed with the few remaining—mainly redneck and hillbilly—supporters he had. No question of walkabouts in places like Los Angeles, for example, where he could expect nothing but vilification and rotten eggs. On a visit to the UK, the only ground he'd dared touch had been that of the helipads outside heavily fortified castles and palaces.

"Tallahassee, right?" said Pferd. "Better watch your step."

"No need…guys and gals down there *lurve* me. Like they should. Now, like I said, get the hell outta my nice hair and do your damn job."

"Sure thing," said Lester, strolling out of the Round Office to take a look at the latest magic ruby stories. "Have a nice trip," he called over his shoulder.

Moments later, he was back on the secret hotline to Igor Ripurpantzov's office. For yes, folks, it was Lester Pferd who was the deepest of Washington DC's deep throats. Not that Igor Ripurpantsov knew his name. As far as he was concerned, Lester was merely a code—XYB749120 GrAb mY PuSsY to be precise. Igor's receiving agent, Rudi Lopurnutzov, was 000020000. KiSs My AsS. It was all very hush hush.

In the circs, however, Igor instructed Rudi in exactly the same manner as Dougal had Lester—i.e. "Get me that jewel before Klank gets his mitts on it"—and the Ruby Race was officially on.

~ * ~

What with all the fuss and bother of recent weeks, Stephanie slept for thirteen more hours than the twenty-four guaranteed by KayCee's fairy blanket and, when she awoke, peered about and screamed. Wouldn't you if your last coherent memory was your house and children. and you suddenly found yourself in a dank cave with dim dream memories of some beach sex party from which you'd been rescued by your newly undead and hopefully soon to be ex-husband? Of course you would.

"Aaaaaaaahhhh," she went, raising herself on an elbow and staring around the barely lit cave containing only a couple more ratty palliasses, a crone combing her lank hair, and a pile of glittering bling topped with a clearly fake ruby the size of a football across which was draped a mini-banner bearing the logo: WHAT IF I RULED THE WORLD.

"So, you're finally awake," said the crone, turning and smiling. "Welcome to my world."

Only she wasn't a crone any longer. In the seconds it had taken her to turn and smile, she'd morphed into the spit of a young Kate Moss.

"Huh-huh-who're *you*?" Stephanie gurgled.

"I am many things," KayCee replied. "Right now, I'm a fashion modely sort of a person, but if you'd like me to be somebody else, I am at your disposal. Just name your preference."

Stephanie buried her head under her fairy blanket, pinched herself, and screamed again. This had to be just one more part of the ongoing nightmare. But how to stop it, that was the question. She screamed even harder when the Kate Moss creature sashayed across the cave catwalk-style, reached inside the blanket, stroked her forehead and muttered the words: "Come thee back, sweet thing. Come thee back and all manner of things shall be well, harrumty, harrum."

And in moments, Stephanie came back, sat up, returned the ex-crone's smile and said, "Pleased to meet you, I'm Stephanie."

~ * ~

Back at number forty-eight Salubrious Place, James had put the kettle on as requested by the peculiar creature claiming to be his elder brother, but made sure in doing so, he took Gabi with him to the kitchen. William barely noticed their absence as, on hands and knees, he gave Nelly the Elephant rides to Ernest and Georgina, who didn't seem to notice he had a different body.

"Nelly the elephant packed her trunk and said goodbye to the circus," he yodeled with both children astride his back. "Off she went with a trumpety, trumpety, trump, *TRUMP, TRUMP, TRUMP*," he continued at which moment he arched his back and tossed them both onto a convenient sofa where they laughed themselves silly and asked for a repeat performance.

Which suited Gabi and James just fine, because it gave them all the time they needed to call distant cousin Norbert on the secure line he'd given them and ask him if he'd mind popping round to help them check out a particularly weird occurrence. No need for the PI work in search of William any more, Gabi told him, because William had just turned up out of nowhere and was playing with his kids. But she and James would be grateful for the advice (and possibly muscles) of one conversant with the ways of the criminal underworld should things turn nasty and push come to shove. This was, after all, the same William who'd supposedly been banged up after the horrendous dystopian abstract nudes roof display and was now playing silly games with his children. Who was to say *what* would happen if he suddenly reverted to his bad old ways?

"*Kein Problem, Gabichen* (No problem, little Gabi)," said Norbert, who arrived at Salubrious Place in what seemed to James and Gabi like no more than two shakes of a cat's tail, saying he'd been in the neighbourhood anyway.

"What can I do to help?" he said, when James opened the door.

"It's William," he whispered. "He's *here*," he added pointing into the lounge area.

"Ah hah," said Norbert, who'd been taking on-line lessons to improve his English. "Would you like me to talk to him?"

"What about?" asked Gabi.

"His plans, short- and long-term. Before I do, however, may I ask if either of you has ever had any connections with elves around these parts?"

"*Elves?*" Gabi's eyes widened, and her jaw dropped.

"You know, mischievous little metamorphic chaps who rather enjoy playing funny tricks on us humans," said Norbert, eyeing James who had taken to scrupulously examining his fingernails for excess length.

"*Elves?*" Gabi repeated.

Norbert nodded towards James. "It's just that I recently stumbled across a trans one called KayCee who claimed to have had meetings with…"

James decided his shoelaces needed re-tying and almost fell over in the process.

Following her distant cousin's gaze, Gabi frowned. "James," she said, "is there something you haven't told me?"

"Um…erm…" said her husband, clutching at a shelf for balance.

"Do not blame him, Gabichen," said Norbert, seeing the distress. "As I understand it, KayCee swore James to silence on fear of death should he ever mention her/his name in your presence. Is that not so, James?"

"Yuh-yuh-yes. Exactly. Fear of death."

"And you both be*lieve*d this was an elf?" said Gabi, staring at the two grown men, who both nodded.

"You should see the tricks he or she can do," Norbert said. "I say 'he or she' because s/he cleverly straddles the normal genders. *Very* impressive. *Any*way, before I speak to your William, there's a little secret I wish to share with you. It comes with KayCee's prior consent, of course."

"We're all ears," muttered Gabi, cupping her ears thespianly.

"Cynicism ill becomes you, little cousin," said Norbert in German before, in English, outlining the plan KayCee had proposed for reuniting William with his family and, for once and for all, bringing total peace to St Ives by ridding it of its scourge of all the remaining HAH-recalcitrant ruby hunters, including the new addition of surly American and Russian faux beach bums and artists sent by Klank's and Ripurpantzov's double-dealing special agents, Pferd and Lopurnutzov.

"S/he could *do* that?" said James once Norbert had sketched the outlines of the plan.

Norbert shrugged. "S/he has recently been doing a little thinking and come to the conclusion now is the time to stop playing both sides against the centre, or being mischievous for its own sake, and decide whether to be only good or only naughty."

"And s/he chose?" said James.

"To be good. S/he even has a little extra project to deal with the Yanks' and Ruskies' bosses back home, but that's still at its pipe-dream stage."

Even Gabi feigned enthusiasm. "Wow. And when would all this happen?"

"Just as soon as feasible," Norbert was saying as William/Nelly the Elephant trundled into their midst with Ernest and Georgina on his back.

"Wazzup, guys?" he said in what he thought of as American. "And who's *this*?" he added, tipping the giggling children onto the floor and jabbing a finger into Norbert's chest.

"Somebody with a deep interest in dystopian abstract nudes, William. You can call me Norbert."

"As in Not Bert Either?" said William, chuckling at what he evidently considered clever wordplay and causing James and Gabi to wince.

It wasn't the best of starts to a relationship, but neither Norbert's English nor his German sense of humour was up to such witticisms, so he just smirked a bit and asked if anybody might make him a cup of tea.

Eighteen

On his first day back at work after scraping through the last of his psychological profiling tests by a mere one percentile point, DI Horace Skewes was surprised indeed to be, yet again, confronted by Cornish Commissioner of Police, K.C.Cardynham, who had somehow managed to materialize in his office before he'd even had time to activate his new "Sorry I'm Out" sign.

"Oh, gosh, wow, what a pleasure, Missus," he said.

"'Commissioner' to you, DI Skewes. So they let you out, I see."

"Nothing wrong with me in the first place. Just a little bang on the head."

"About time you grew a pair though, eh?"

"Of heads?" said Skewes, who was as unfamiliar with street argot as he was with the streets themselves.

"Of balls. *Anyway*, enough of the jollity and down to business, eh?"

"What business?"

"You may or may not remember that before your delusion testing you were involved in the murder case of William Cockburn?"

"Of course I bloody remember. The bloke with the same head but a different body," said Skewes, blinking, paling, and quivering slightly.

"Seen telly pictures of him while I was banged up, didn't I? Falling off some building he was. Only, he wasn't dead then either."

"How very perceptive of you, Detective Inspector. Now, if you would be so kind, I would be grateful if you would provide me with the keys to your morgue."

Skewes baulked at this. "Sorry, Missus, I can't just…"

Cardynham raised an eyebrow, squared her shoulders, and cocked her head over the left one.

"Unless, of course, you would prefer an*other* short course of brain investigation with perhaps the additive of a little-pair-growing hormone treatment? It would be easy for me to arrange. Just a click of my fingers is all it would take, and…"

It would be fun to report the keys to the morgue were in the "Commissioner's" hands before she could say boo to a baboon, but it took Skewes's skewed neurons a little longer than that to recall where the keys were, remember the combination of the safe wherein they were kept—six failed attempts at that—distinguish the morgue keys from those for the bicycle sheds, cells, VIP lavatories, and the secret stash of dope taken from pushers and kept for special St Ives PD parties, before his fumbling fingers finally lit on those requested. Let's say it was more like forty-eight boos to an increasingly tetchy baboon, during which KayCee/Cardynham harrumphed a lot.

But finally, the job was done and, leaving Skewes immediately to activate his *Catch 22* Major Major Major sign and head for the window, the once mischievous-turned-newly-benevolent elf was back on the street with the keys in his/her hand to meet William who was loitering as inconspicuously as he was able—which wasn't *very* inconspicuously—on the pavement outside the cop shop. Already, he'd given interviews to seven passing dystopian abstract nude fans and signed their autograph books, which didn't please KayCee one jot.

"Some *dick* you still can be," s/he told him. "But I've got the keys, so follow me. Like *behind* me with this bag over your head?" s/he added when William started striding off in front of her.

~ * ~

Stephanie returned to the homestead a wiser and happier woman. Back in the cave, before releasing William to visit his children, and then marching him off to the cop shop prior to his body swap, KayCee in his/her new guise as good fairy had given both him and Stephanie a stern lecture about human gender distinctions and their pitfalls, especially within marriage.

"Don't get me wrong, I'm no feminist. Nor, however, am I a masculinist," s/he'd begun as William and Stephanie sat before her like naughty schoolchildren. "Unlike you humans, we elves do not believe in such paltry and misleading distinctions. We are, as you might have noticed, gender neutral."

"You mean you're all trans gays?" said William with what he thought of as wit, but KayCee dismissed as pusillanimity.

"Typically human," s/he sighed. "Always so ready to categorize. No wonder you're all so screwed up. *No*, we are *not* 'trans gays.' Like you humans when in the embryonic stage although you fail to recognize it, we are always already partly male and partly female and remain so because we have no desire to jump definitively one way or the other. We just are what we *are*. Bits of both."

William gawped, but Stephanie nodded.

"I can see the sense in that," she said.

"And what do you think it means in practice?" asked KayCee,

"In the fairy world?"

"Of course in the fairy world, where else?"

William gawped some more, particularly when his wife came up with the right answer.

"That you don't bother with gender distinctions because there's no need."

KayCee smiled. "Spot on. Of course we don't."

"And if there's no difference between the sexes, there are no power games specific to either, no gender-fiction rules to abide by. Which would probably make marriages a lot easier."

"Quite so. Mind you, young woman, in Fairyland such is the case in *all* aspects of life, not just in what you call marriage, which we don't need, anyway. The same is true in the workplace, and on the sports field, as well as in the home, because all elves are born equal, and none ever becomes more equal than any other, including our dear leader, Brosista Oberoni, who is sworn to the maintenance of equal ops across the board."

"You mean…?" queried William in disbelief. "There's nothing to say a man has certain undeniable privileges around the place?" he added before falling back on the crusty old chestnut of males being the hunters who brought home the family's meat, which the females cooked.

KayCee grimaced. "Such bullshit. Apart from anything, we elves do not eat our fellow animals any more than we eat each other."

It was Stephanie's turn to smile. "No law of the jungle then?"

"How could there be?" said KayCee before moving the argument along more pertinently to the ways in which s/he proposed William and Stephanie might in future co-exist…in harmony as both opposites *and* equals.

"You mean we should just remove the whole of human history at a stroke and begin all over again?" William protested.

"It could be a place to start," KayCee agreed. "It's not as if dystopian abstract nudes have exactly put much food on *your* family's table, is it?"

William turned puce, balled his fists like a baby—or the CEO of USA. Inc.—and looked prepared for a proper tantrum until KayCee steepled his/her fingers, interlocked the second ones, twisted both hands around so the interlocked ones waggled, muttered the magic words extropool/looportxe and cast upon William the spell that would pacify and eradicate his sexist furies.

Stephanie was impressed, especially when her newly undead husband with the wrong body calmed down, fell on bended knees, and apologized for having been such a twatish male chauvinist boar all his life. There would be some future re-emergences of such deeply engrained boarish twatishness—vide the episode outside the cop shop after KayCee got the morgue keys from Skewes, for example—but generally speaking William was on the road to a fresh start in life.

"Do I get the same spell, too?" asked Stephanie.

"No, no, my dear. I doubt you need it. Now, let's get this show on the road, shall we?"

And so it was that William was released from the cave for the Nelly the Elephant performance with Ernest and Georgina, and when somewhat later Stephanie returned home, she was a wiser and happier woman.

~ * ~

With William having been whisked away from them by KayCee on their morgue body-snatch expedition, Stephanie, Gabi, James and Norbert were left together at forty-eight Salubrious Place to try and fit together the jigsaw pieces of the peculiar events unfolding around them and complete the picture. Of the quartet, it was only Gabi who had yet to meet the elf variously known as Koleen, Chucklebutty and K.C. Cardynham, and she it was who remained the most suspicious of his/her intervention in their lives, jigsaw completion or no jigsaw completion.

"You are not seriously suggesting," she told the group over a dinner of an excellent spaghetti Bolognese cooked by Norbert, "that the woman police commissioner who just called here for William was an *elf*, and we are all living some fairy tale."

Refreshing their glasses with a vintage Pilastro Primitivo red wine, Norbert shrugged and nodded, as did James and Stephanie who, although having known KayCee in different manifestations, were unable to deny his/her otherworldly existence. But Gabi remained unconvinced.

"And what were you on when you made her acquaintance? Grass? Cocaine? Heroin? *fairy* potion?"

More shrugging from the neophytes, all of whom denied any use of mind-enhancers in their dealings with KayCee and gave credibly sober accounts of their experiences. Of James's and Stephanie's we already know, which leaves the most improbable of the lot, Norbert's.

"It was many, many years ago in nineteen eighty-nine. Back in the bad old days of East Berlin when I was young and even more foolish than I later became or am now," he began before going on to recount his meeting with the elf who, in those days, called him/herself Brunhilde, daughter of Odin, and who promised him untold wealth if he would do one small favour for her.

Gabi stared. "When you were a Stasi officer?"

"When I was a Stasi officer of the worst kind."

"And the favour?"

"Before I tell you, you must know it was Brunhilde who was to play the greatest, yet never revealed, role in the fall of The Wall. In those days, too, she was the good fairy, you see."

"Are...you...*crazy*?" muttered Gabi. "The wall fell because of the two Gees, glasnost and Gorbachev."

"That's what the world was given to believe, cousin. But, trust me, Brunhilde had more to do with it than any human politician."

"And your small favour?"

"Was to infiltrate the *Volkspolizei*'s high command with fake news of rebellions in the very south of the zone such that when the guards who patrolled The Wall suddenly found themselves free to climb over it and into the West they could, because the guards who guarded *them* had all been drafted south. You will remember the guards who guarded the guards with orders to shoot them dead should they make any false moves."

Gabi did. Her father had been one of them.

"And you are saying it was you who changed history by...?"

"Not me. I swear to you it was the Brunhilde I met in a bar on the Friedrichstraße. I was only one of her many pawns."

"Who then became a criminal mastermind?"

"To my shame, yes. But by then, I was no longer in touch with Brunhilde. It was only last week when I first arrived in St Ives that she came back into my life after all these years. Purely by accident as I was strolling the beach. No longer called Brunhilde, of course. The name she gave me was KayCee, but after all his/her years of mischief, it was clear to me who the fairy was, and that s/he was back with another beneficent agenda."

"Which was?"

"You would be prepared to let me explain?"

Gabi nodded reluctantly and, teetering on capitulation, her final acquiescence was abetted by brat senior Ernest the Earnest who, unbeknownst to anybody, had crept out of the bed he was supposed to be sleeping in and from an upstairs landing had listened in to all the grown-ups' "fairy" tales.

"From my not inconsiderable research into all matters supernatural," he announced from halfway down the stairs, "elves are for real and should never be disbelieved. I could provide a long list of examples should you so desire."

Gabi laughed. She couldn't help it, as Ernest in his pyjamas trundled over to his mother's lap and nestled in it.

Stephanie smiled awkwardly. "He's always been a bit, you know…"

"Clever?" said Gabi.

"He's nobody's fool," said his mother.

"Should I tell them what I know, Mummy?"

Stephanie checked with the others for the go-ahead, which came without demur—even from Gabi.

So, to Norbert's gratification in particular, Ernest started on a fifteen-minute exegesis of elfdom based largely on Benjamin Radford's *A History of Elves* which chronicled tales of their exploits from the fifteen century to the present day and left Ernest in no doubt of their existence.

"It's a jolly good documentary," he concluded to a spontaneous outburst of applause from all those in the room, after which he took a brief bow then, at his mother's behest, headed back to bed.

James was astonished and quickly upgraded his estimation of Ernest from "brat" to "brainbox."

"So, Gabi, are you now persuaded?" Norbert said.

"As far as I'll ever be. So, cousin of mine, do continue."

And so it was that Norbert outlined the parts of KayCee's plan he knew for sure, the ones James and a disbelieving Gabi had already heard, the first of which was the restoration of William's family role, albeit with a "new and improved" mindset dedicated less to the promotion of himself and his dystopian abstract nudes and more to Stephanie and the kids. To which, Nobert added the swap back to William's old body after the morgue snatch expedition with KayCee.

"And he will forgive my little peccadilloes at the beach party?" asked Stephanie.

"KayCee has already wiped them from his mind," Norbert assured her. "To him, it is now *he* who was ever the wrongdoer, and *you* who are utterly guiltless. A nifty switch, *nicht wahr*?"

Stephanie bit her lower lip to stop it from smiling.

"My old William back with me," she said.

"Indeed," said Norbert. "But not so much of the 'old.' The new and improved version will see you with entirely different eyes. He will also have plans for a far better relationship than ever before with you, James, and seek to heal any recent misunderstandings between yourself and your good lady wife, my cousin Gabi," he added, causing James to smirk.

"New and improved, eh?" he said. "Like some soap powder. A bit difficult to be 'new' *and* 'improved' though, would you not say? Either it's *entirely* new or just the old one tarted up with a different niff."

Still lacking a British sense of humour, Norbert missed the joke and merely assured James this would be a "better" brother he'd be dealing with, at which James shrugged and took to whistling Buddy Holly's "That'll Be The Day." Gabi nudged him, smiled, and said, "Let us wait and see, shall we?"

Undeterred, Norbert went on to outline the second of KayCee's plans, viz peace for St Ives through the removal of the "power ruby" from its cave to an unknown destination which would be hyper-advertised on all print, TV, and social media.

"Nothing to find, nothing to gain, nothing to fight over," he concluded to nods of appreciation all around.

"And that's it, that's *all*?" said Gabi. "I thought there was some other thing on the elf's mind. Something to do with the White House and the Kremlin?"

"Ah, *that*," said Norbert, "is still at the drawing board stage. When I hear different, you'll be the first to know. But if KayCee was able to engineer the peace that broke out between the two parts of Germany left over after nineteen forty-five, I'd put money on a successful outcome to his or her current strategy. You can put your mortgage on KayCee when such an elf has a plan brewing."

Nineteen

KayCee and William waited until the dead of night to approach the gates of St Ives morgue in order not to draw unnecessary attention.

"Shhhhhh!" KayCee told her charge when he started giggling. "Are you crazy?" she added, fumbling for the keys in his/her elf satchel.

"Sure, a little. Wouldn't you be if your body was about to be swapped?"

"My body has been swapped so many times over the centuries, I don't remember the original one." S/he chuckled, still fumbling.

But then the keys to the morgue were suddenly in her/his hand and selecting the largest—the one that should fit the outer gates, s/he reckoned—s/he tried inserting it into the lock. Twice s/he tried. Three times. But however hard s/he tried it...would...not...*fit*.

"Oh for *FUCK*," s/he said, causing William to cock his head, waggle a forefinger, tut tut, and say, "Now, now, good fairies don't swear, do they?"

"This one fucking well does when the key that was supposed to open the fucking morgue gates is the one for the fucking police gymnasium," s/he said. "That's what it says on the fob label. That Skewes, the next time I see him I'm gonna..."

"Chew his balls off and fry them up with eggs for breakfast?"

"At the very least," said KayCee, checking the other two keys, one of which read Lockers and the other Showers. "What...a...*fuck*wit."

"Doo calmio, doo calmio, ma petite," said William in what he thought of as French.

Which, surprising even him, worked.

"You're right. There's always an alternative, *n'est ce pas?*"

"Always, elfie. As I now know only too well."

KayCee smiled and took his hand. "So it's back to plan B."

"Which is?"

"Magic, my friend. Always useful as a last resort. Or sometimes, a first resort. Now then," s/he said, wafting across the morgue gates a little wand s/he took from the fairy satchel and incanting the words, "wooshie swooshie little gaties, open for mummy."

Which worked a treat. Within microseconds, the cast iron defences slid noiselessly open to reveal a short, weed-infested pathway leading to a heavy oaken door bearing the logo, "Death Is Final."

"Yeah, yeah," said KayCee, "We'll see about that. Prepare yourself for a little more sorcery, young William. The door I'm sure I can open, but behind that there will be a guard."

"Want me to biff him?" said William, flexing the muscles of the Muhammad Ali body he was about to lose in favour of the old one he'd been born with.

KayCee laughed. "You could try, but frankly I'd prefer my option."

"Which is?"

"A spell equivalent in strength to more morphine than it would take to fell a raging bull and calm it into a whimpering gelder."

"You could *do* that?"

"Watch me."

And so it was that KayCee and William broke into the morgue, left "Corpse Officer" Clive Carew comatose at his post, and made their way into the sub-zero refrigerated room containing all the corpse drawers each conveniently labeled with its ex-owner's name.

~ * ~

In Washington DC, Dougal Klank was hanging on to his presidency by a pubic hair. Legion were the court cases, the White House insider reports of unstable and moronic behaviour, the accusations of association with the Kremlin and corrupt business practices, and the claims from WAK (Women Against Klank) that he had become terminally impotent, and, anyway, had a willy so small and floppy it had to be clamped in a special brace to make it stand up at all. But even these harbingers of doom paled into insignificance in light of *The Washington Gazette's* latest claims—verified by the deepest of the White House's deep throats—that the president went to bed in a frilly pink nightgown and had been seen propped up on purple pillows eating a live hamster called Norman. There were many things for which the average American redneck or hillbilly Klank supporter was prepared to forgive, or even praise in their hero's "little missteps," but going to bed in a frilly pink nightgown wasn't one of them.

"Holy shit, you figure the guy for a *fag*?" was the question being asked all the way up the spine of America in diners from El Paso to Detroit by folk named Chuck and Lulubelle, for example. "Man, last time I ever vote me in a fag to be prez. God said it weren't right bein' a fag, ain't that right? An' He wrote the bible, so He should know."

"Damn right, Chuck," the Lulubelles would reply. And then, naturally, their thoughts exploded all over the Twitterverse in which thousands of *other* Chucks and Lulubelles found themselves equally "disgusted."

Dougal wasn't pleased. Not in the least he wasn't.

"Get me the enemy of the people, fake news freak who wrote that goddam horseshit, an' I will fire his ass from here to planet Zplink," he roared at Lester Pferd, who reckoned that wasn't the time to tell his boss *he* was the one who'd okayed the story, and also, there was no planet called Zplink.

"Frilly *pink* nightgown, for crissakes," roared Klank, tugging at his toupée. "Blue I could live with, but *PINK*."

Lester also reckoned that wasn't the time further to raise the matter of live hamster eating which had been barely mentioned by the rednecks and hillbillies except for the protests of RAHALHE (Rednecks and Hillbillies Against Live Hamster Eating), and a tiny group of hamster lovers in Grand Island Nebraska. The frilly pink nightgown story he'd leaked would have to suffice. Instead, he attempted to move the conversation along to the upbeat.

"That ruby you wanted me to get?" he tried. "The one in Cornfield England?" Lester's grasp of world geography wasn't much better than Klank's.

But Dougal was still fixated on the nightgown issue. Some said once he was fixated, it could take days to get him refocused, which wasn't very focused in the first place. Wars could start, economies could collapse, hurricanes could drown whole populations as a result of the climate change he anyway denied, but Dougal wouldn't give a shit if his amour propre—"*im*proper love" as some *New York Times* wits had dubbed it—had been offended. Even as Lester spoke, he was already shooting himself in the foot with a volley of tweets denying all knowledge of nightgowns of any colour, especially outsize teddies from an online site whose address he supplied.

"A customer, huh? An' he sure as hell don't normally go for fat broads," the Chucks and Lulubelles across the nation would mutter, thus reducing Dougal's popularity rating by the thirty-two percent that would take it into negative territory for the first time in American presidential history.

However, all that was still to come. Meanwhile, Lester plugged away at the World Power Ruby issue on which, as it happened, he had genuine news in the form of a hyper-encrypted email from someone called Casey in Cornwall England saying the ruby was on sale on the open market to the highest bidder with bids starting at the knock-down price of a mere thousand dollars or sixty-eight thousand rubles.

But was the CEO of USA Inc. interested? The hell he was.

"Nightgowns! For...*fuck's*...sake," he said, jabbing away at his smartphone with one stubby finger transmitting syntactical and lexical errata with every jab.

Igor Ripurpantsov was very amused by the whole incident when it was recounted to him by XYB749120 GrAb mY PuSsY Rudi Lopurnutzov. Mind you, unlike nightgown fetishist and live hamster eater Klank, he *was* interested in the ruby auction, albeit he had no intention of paying the asking price of sixty-eight thousand rubles.

No siree, theft was more the name of Igor's game, possibly with a few unprovable novichok murders thrown in for good measure. Why pay for what you could get for free was the mantra Igor had lived by ever since stealing as many of the ex-USSR's fossil fuel reserves as he could get his hands on in the naughty nineteen nineties.

~ * ~

By comparison with KayCee's surgical skills, modern medicine is left languishing in the doldrum days of the sawbones, particularly, when it comes to whole-body transplants. Okay, such operations are rarely, if ever, conducted anywhere in the world, but should they ever be required, KayCee would be the person to consult. Mind you, s/he would probably be a whizz at triple heart by-passes and other lesser procedures with patients in and out of hospital in a few minutes, beating keyhole surgery by a country mile. Not that s/he's ever likely to share her knowledge with humans because elves are sworn by their version of the Hippocratic oath *never* to interfere in human health affairs except *in extremis* for fear of upsetting too many apple carts. In the case of William Cockburn, however—having already broken elf law by body-swapping him one way—s/he had little alternative but to break it again with the reverse procedure. Which would have gone a whole lot faster if William hadn't been such a scaredy pants. It wasn't as though finding his old body was hard. The label on the morgue freezer drawer was quite clear, as was the one belonging to the body he had acquired in the previous op. "William Jocelyn Cockburn" and "Dennis 'The Slugger' Dickens," they said.

(Dennis had been Cornwall's heavyweight boxing champion until his cardiac arrest during a failed attempt to win the national title).

No problem at all, therefore, for KayCee to open the drawers with a waft of his/her wand and the magic words "Nepo, nepo, little rezeerf sreward. Dennis's was empty apart from his head, obviously enough, seeing as William was wearing its previous body contents, but there in William's lay his headless *old* body—at the sight of which William paled, screamed, broke into a mega-cold sweat and, understandably, fainted. I mean how would *you* fancy seeing your ex-body frozen like a slab of meat in a six-foot cube of ice?

But KayCee was unimpressed. "Oh, for Titania's sake snap out of it, we haven't got all night," s/he said. "It's only your own body."

But there was no reaction from William. KayCee tried poking him with needles and yelling in his ear but still no response. S/he could, of course, have awakened him with another of her spells, but thinking on his/her feet as always, s/he calculated a blackout to be potentially every bit as effective as an anaesthetic and, with the insurance of an extra elf message to sleep till she woke him, went to work.

The steps she took were these:

Step one: To remove William's lanky ex-body from the drawer, lay it on a convenient trolley, then to thaw it out and resuscitate it with a special elf blood transfusion procedure, another waft of her/his wand and the magic words wakety, wakety, ydob. Which worked yet another treat. In a flash, the torso and limbs took to twitching and looking set to go.

"Ookey, dokey," KayCee muttered before moving on to step two, which was to return to William's prone form, from which s/he separated the head with a special elf scalpel then hurry back to the twitching body on the trolley, lay the head with perfect symmetry against the pulsating neck, waft the wand again, and pronounce the words "Ydob, Ydob, now be whole again," at which the old William sat up with a jerk, stared down at his real old self, and took to weeping.

"I duh-duh-don't luh-luh-*like* it," he moaned.

"Well you're stuck with it, sunshine. That was the deal, right?" said KayCee over his/her shoulder as s/he shifted poor old Dennis's powerful frame back into his drawer, muttered the magic words, "Tuhs, tuhs, little rezeerf sreward," at which both Dennis's and William's freezer drawers slid silently shut.

"Now, let's get the hell outta here before any alarm bells ring," s/he told a still lacrimose William, jerking him to his (original natal) feet in a full nelson then shoving him towards the exit. "The last thing we need right now is coppers breathing down our necks."

And so it was that, with difficulty and a lot of whimpering, William Cockburn was returned to his family in what would have been his birthday suit if KayCee hadn't been thoughtful enough to come equipped with a change of clothes four sizes smaller than the ones he'd arrived in. Dennis Dickens had been a *lot* bigger than William, which was possibly why William was warbling like the newborn he more or less was.

"For mercy's sake, shut it and try to smile, will you?" KayCee told him as they approached number forty-eight Salubrious Place where, at precisely the appointed hour of six-thirty a.m., Stephanie, Ernest, Georgina, James, Gabi, and Norbert were waiting to welcome them.

Twenty

KayCee/Casey had no intention of auctioning off the "world-power" ruby for however much money. S/he had merely been on a little phishing trip with her emails on the subject to see who might be crazy enough to be caught in her trawl. It still astonished him/her that humans continued to fall into such traps, especially those of them dumb enough to swallow the bait of the thirty-eight trillion dollar fortune with their name written on it hidden away in some Shanghai bank account by an until then unheard-of relative. But swallow they did. And all they had to do was to provide their bank details and the necessary ID codes and the fortune would be theirs.

"Duh!" was KayCee's response to *that*, as well as to the phone calls and sometimes house visits from jazzy/plummy-voiced men and women claiming to be police, smartphone company reps, bank managers, tax inspectors etc, all of them requiring the same info if citizens/customers wanted to stay out of jail on a murder charge, salvage their cloned phone from the hands of terrorists, avoid the impending withdrawal of their credit cards and freezing of their accounts as a temporary, but necessary, precaution against a threatened worldwide hack, or not have to pay the million pound fine for tax evasion in the offshore account they didn't have.

"Duh! Duh!" All it took was a little common sense and/or research—particularly if they hadn't killed anybody this week, had a different smartphone from the model mentioned, or belonged to a different bank than the one facing the hacking menace. But no, no, on they went dishing out their personal details like confetti to the bride from hell.

"Dud! Duh! Duh!" In Fairyland, such nonsense could never happen. But this was the human zone where it happened all the time; the Facebook world in which you were nobody unless thousands of fictitious "friends" "liked" you. So, feeling no guilt, KayCee/Casey exploited what was there for the taking, using power as the even more tempting lure than money. And even s/he was astonished at the volume of replies s/he received: three million, nine hundred thousand, five hundred and sixty-seven in a single thirty-minute exposure according to the instantaneous response of the special calculometer attached to his/her ElfMoc computer.

"Wowee," s/he muttered as the screen filled up with even more bidders, some already hiking the offered price to three million US dollars. Not that s/he would waste time opening them all, of course. Far too boring that would be. Using her remote SuperSampler, however, s/he took a few random peeks to get a feel for the world power seekers out there and was astonished to find they weren't just the tin-pot dictators of crap countries on the verge of terminal bankruptcy s/he'd expected. Yes, there were a few of those, plus several (very) elder statespersons who clearly reckoned this to be their last chance at global dominion, and what the hell did they have to lose? And of course, there was a whole slew of Wall Street-type master of the universe wannabes, but KayCee was astonished at the numbers of male and female bus drivers, general practitioners, garbage disposal officers, garage mechanics, neurosurgeons, failed X-Factor contestants, and people on state benefits who saw themselves as worthy of wielding such global influence. One such was a John Lennon lookalike from Toxteth Liverpool who sang "Imagine" along with his bid of one thousand pounds and one penny, and a note saying how he'd change the world if he won. It was signed "Peace, Love, and Power to the People. Pete."

Shaking her head in wonder, KayCee concluded this sample of respondents was either mentally disturbed—a strong possibility—or just thought they'd been playing the latest computer game.

"Sheeesh!" s/he said before re-setting the Elf InstaProg to its Specific Select mode in which it could pick out respondents in whom KayCee was particularly interested, the names, pseudonyms, and even top secret code addresses which s/he had sourced from TEHDONPAETSCA (The Elf Hyper Dictionary of Names, Pseudonyms, and even Top Secret Code Addresses).

And bingo, when s/he typed in the names s/he was most interested in—the both-way-leaning Pferd in Washington DC, and his equally nasty equivalent Lopurnutzov in The Kremlin—up they both popped.

"Yippee," trilled KayCee, dancing a little known elf dance called The Pixy Pirouette in the cave recently vacated by Stephanie and William and winking at the magic ruby, which winked back in anticipation of its coming role in world politics.

Then, she called Norbert on a hyper secure line to let him know they were in business.

~ * ~

On his return home, nobody at forty-eight Salubrious Street mentioned William's double body transplant. Why? Because, on KayCee's advice, Norbert had told the adults it would be better psychologically speaking to pretend it had never happened.

"Let him believe it was just a dream, it will be less painful that way," s/he'd explained to Norbert. "Such was the spell I cast upon him during the operation."

"And the dystopian abstract nudes antics on the rooftop?"

"An oneiric wish-fulfilment experience, all evidence of which I have been careful to erase."

So this was the message passed on to Stephanie, James, and Gabi. Ernest and Georgina never noticed the difference, anyway, because Stephanie had been careful to shield them from their father's shenanigans by telling them Daddy had been away at an art conference in Spain. They were a bit surprised he wasn't tanned, but James said that was because it wasn't always sunny in Spain.

"Yes, Spanish rain falls on plains quite a lot," Ernest confirmed Professor Henry Higgins-ishly.

"Indeed," said William, blissfully unaware of events during his absence from the homestead. "What a *clever* little chap you are, Ernest. And such a nice singing voice."

Ernest shrugged off the compliment, but a surprised Stephanie smiled. In his previous incarnation, William had barely paid any attention to his children even when he was at home, which was rarely, given he had to devote so much of his time to painting and romancing his dystopian abstract nude models at the studio.

"And how's my darling little girl?" he went on to ask Georgina, taking her in his arms and cuddling her so hard her eyes popped and—a still smiling—Stephanie had to wrestle her away.

It was all very heart-warming. James was astonished, particularly when later over lunch his big brother laid an arm around his shoulder and asked, without any sarcasm, how the writing was coming along.

"Anything new on the drawing board?" he said. "Possibly about time to break untrodden ground, eh? Pretty innovative your stuff has been so far, but possibly time to move away from the autobiog stories of the poor boy nobody loves?" he added with a brother-in-law type of a wink at Gabi. No lust in the wink at all.

It was Gabi's turn to smile. "Good idea, William. I've been suggesting much the same thing myself. Perhaps something with a wider range—politics and fantasy in the mix, who knows?"

James blushed.

"That true, old chap?"

"Well...um...you know, William...I might have a bash."

"Modest as always. And do let us drop the 'William,' shall we? From here on in I shall be 'Bill.'"

"Okay...*Bill*," said James, tasting the name and rather liking it.

Norbert looked on and grinned. The first part of KayCee's promised metamorphic plan, the family one, looked as if it was working out just fine, and there was no reason to think it might not continue, and not only in relation to those in William's ambit. Having warmed to his long lost distant cousin Gabi, Norbert had also put in a special plea that her relationship with James might move into smoother waters, to which KayCee had winked, and said s/he would do what s/he could. Which must have been quite a lot, to judge from the coochy cooing the pair were increasingly doing, *and*, unless Norbert was very much mistaken, from the unusual thickening around Gabi's waistline. Knowing KayCee as he did, s/he would probably have a stork or two ready and waiting in the wings.

He was also pleased to see the second item on the agenda coming to fruition as the streets, beaches, and hostelries of St Ives returned to their old peaceful ways once the rival ruby hunters finally disbanded and dispersed back whither they'd come. He could only assume when announcing its auction, that KayCee had also made it clear the valuable item was so securely locked away pending sale that nobody would ever find it. That or its potential buyers had called off the dogs on the assumption they would be able legally to buy it instead. Whatever the case, the results were pleasing indeed. So there was still a good fairy hidden away in KayCee after all, just like the one he'd known all those decades ago in Berlin, the one who had helped change the world.

And, to judge from the chirpy call Norbert had received saying they were in business on the ruby auction game, the third part of KayCee's plan looked to be in place, too. He just wished s/he would tell him precisely what it was. If Berlin were anything to go by, it had to be pretty momentous, but Norbert could only guess at its parameters. God only knew there were enough calamities waiting to happen on the planet, but which had KayCee elected to confront this time?

"Mmm," he muttered to himself, watching on as "Bill" sauntered off into the kitchenette after Stephanie to help her wash the lunch dishes for what would be the first time in their married life.

"And when we're done, how about we take the kids for a stroll down along the beach? Donkey rides and ice-creams?" he called over his shoulder. "You and Gabi be up for that, Jimmy? And you, too, of course, Norbert."

They all nodded, "Jimmy" in particular. The name made him sound so much younger and less serious. Also, it was a whole lot better than the "Fart Face" his big brother had called him when they were kids.

And the stroll went well. Everybody had fun. Watching events on the ElfVision monitor, KayCee chuckled. S/he liked it when a plan came together. Sitting alongside, Ruby chuckled, too, as she awaited the signal for action.

Twenty-one

Frustratingly it was at this point—just as s/he had done before the collapse of the Berlin Wall—that KayCee vanished back to Fairyland, leaving humans to figure out the ensuing chain of events for themselves. Which was a big ask for such tiny brains, hence the plethora of hypotheses, all fantastical, that poured forth across the globe to explain the sudden disappearance from it of Dougal Klank and Igor Ripurpantzov. The media, social and otherwise, were ablaze with stories, but none could be substantiated, and so the chatter went on with "eye witness" accounts of final sightings of the world's nastiest leaders, many of which were accurate but gave no clue as to what had *happened* to them.

"Last I saw of him he was taking a piss—squeezin' like hell—in the White House john," reported secretary of state Maxwell "Wild Bill" Hickok of his final encounter with Klank. "An' he was, like, super happy because he'd just gotten some jewel he'd rilly, rilly wanted. After that, I dunno. He just kinda dematerialized from the scene."

Dougal had also been seen, or rather felt on that final day, by his latest press secretary Yvonne O'Shea. "Felt" because she was pretty sure it had been he who had crept up behind her while she was looking out of one of the Round Office's windows and grabbed her ass before scooting behind his desk and pretending to sign yet another presidential edict that wouldn't work.

"He was always after my ass an' more if he could get it," Yvonne told *The Washington Enquirer*. "I knew it was him from the type of grab, like with the middle finger going through to the front? Braggin' he was a world ruler, he was. But then he was gone an' I never saw him again. Like he was some ghost. Very weird."

And so it went...on...and on...and on. And not just with final real life sightings. Picking up on Yvonne's spectral image, Dougal was soon being seen on golf courses across America but vanishing every time the viewer got near. Ditto with sundry other locations, all with the same outcome. The only thing that could be said for sure was he no longer existed in anything other than folks' imaginations. Which came as a great relief to all those who'd been trying to impeach him *and* those who feared he would have started World War Three by accident if allowed to carry on as president/CEO of the U.S.A. As to how or why he'd died or disappeared or whatever, they didn't give a rat's ass.

Much the same could be said for Igor Ripurpantzov's Russian detractors. Okay, so one day he was marching around lording it over everybody with his new gem in his lapel, and the next he wasn't, so fucking *what*? Good riddance to bad rubbish was their idea. Given the intense secrecy surrounding the Kremlin, however, it was some time before Igor's failure to show up at meetings, or anywhere else, was disclosed to the Russian public, let alone the wider world. Although, of course, eventually, it had to be, and then came the same spew of stories as for Dougal, except these were KGB- scripted for world consumption. Igor had been last seen skinny-dipping in the lake surrounding his dacha and was presumed drowned. Igor had been spotted overworking himself on his personal gym Mister Macho machines and suffered a heart attack worthy of such a noble leader. Which were all bollocks, of course, because nobody had a clue where (or if) he was.

Meanwhile, it was reported by some of the more imaginative members of the international media that both Dougal and Igor had been abducted by a low flying, probably Martian, UFO while skateboarding at a top-secret venue in Uzbekistan.

Stories, stories, stories, more and more of them cluttering the ether with each passing day. It was a pity, indeed, that KayCee had chosen this moment to return home. But even had s/he stayed, s/he would have obeyed the prime rule of omertà: tell nobody under any circumstances. As did the two humans who'd been involved in the handling of Ruby: XYB749120 GrAb mY PuSsy Lester Pferd and his Moscow equivalent 000020000 KiSs My AsS Rudi Lopurnutzov, both of whom had sworn to Casey he would have the right to kill them both should either give away his identity or admit to *any* knowledge of what had come to pass. It was all totally, absolutely, and utterly sub rosa.

And why exactly had KayCee left the job to mere humans? Because it was *they*, not elves, who had screwed up their planet, and s/he reckoned it was about time they squared up to some responsibility in the matter. Anyway, s/he had other urgent business to attend to in Fairyland whither Brosista Oberoni, the democratically elected leader, had urgently requested her presence to help fight off riotous pressure from a hitherto unknown brand of renegade populist/fascist goblins for him/her to abdicate and hand over power to them. There was no way KayCee could ignore such a request, not when it came from the one—Brosy as s/he called him/her—who'd supervised her/his final elf exams, and, thereafter, granted his/her highest achieving student ever the Freedom of Fairyland.

Anyway, *any*way it was to Lester and Rudi s/he had bequeathed the potentially poisoned chalice of becoming the guardians of the truth when it came to the fates of Dougal Klank and Igor Ripurpantzov— which, for the sake of your inevitable curiosity and with obvious trepidation, *I* now take it upon myself to reveal to you. Not that you're any more likely to believe my account than any of the others offered in explanation. "Just one more piece of fruitcake fiction, most probably," I hear you grumble, and with some justification. But suspend your disbelief for one second, if you would be so good, and let the power of 'what if' have its moment in the sun.

Sitting comfortably? Okay then. So the facts of the matter are these: the first winner of KayCee's ruby auction was Dougal Klank whom, by morphing into an Indonesian man-eating python, Ruby had scoffed whole leaving no remains. Thereafter, back in gem mode, she had been transferred by Lester Pferd to Rudi Lopurnutzov's custody in Moscow, where she performed the same trick on auction runner-up Igor Ripurpantzov, only this time in the form of a starved lioness. One mouthful, a bit of chomping, and that was it—no more Igor except for the rumble in Ruby's tummy, which she soon shat out with the help of three laxative pills and a swig of Igor's vodka. Then, poof, just like that, s/he was gone in a cloud of fairy dust. And *that*, folks, is the true account of the disappearance from Washington DC, and the Kremlin, of the two world leaders most likely to have caused havoc and mayhem amongst us. A blessing in anybody's book and all thanks to the fairy KayCee and her two human helpers, both of whom are now living peaceful, happy, fully incognito lives on sunny islands as yet undocumented on any map.

"Yeah, yeah, sure. And my dad was Muffin the Mule, so go pull the other one," I hear you say. "How the hell do *you* know the truth when nobody else does? Rubies turning into pythons and lions, then eating people? You have got to be outta your freakin' mind."

That's what my (Lacanian) therapist Doctor Magnus McShrinkstein says, too, which is the reason he's diagnosed me with what he terms "Intractable Lunacy" and given me these little green-and-blue-striped pills, but they haven't kicked in yet, and they never will. Why? Because I'm *not* insane, that's why. It's just that I have this telepathic thing going with KayCee. S/he and I are pals. We speak the same language, which is rare between humans and "the other," but I commend it to you. Crazy I may be thought to be but, I like to think, in a nice way. At least, I have eyes that I hope can see. Let us hope they can bring life to thee.

And so ends of the first part of our story, which deals with helpful elvish interventions in the frequently foolish, often downright pernicious behaviour of humans. Now, let us turn our attention to events in Fairyland whither, as you will recall, KayCee had returned to help out her/his old friend and mentor, Brosista Oberoni, with his/her struggles against populist/fascist goblins.

Part Two

Twenty-two

Apart from her Italian Greyhound Cyndy, Brosista dwelt alone in the same tiny hut s/he had occupied since coming to life six hundred and ninety-seven years before in human time, or "some yesterday or another" in elf thinking, seeing as elves don't bother with temporal concepts beyond yesterday, today, and—if pushed—tomorrow. Anything else is too hard to remember or too hard to foresee. Mind you, "alone" didn't mean s/he lived in complete isolation, far from it, just that s/he didn't share the hut with anybody else except Cyndy and the occasional lover. Otherwise, she was kept company by a regular flow of visitors from all over Fairyland, mainly envoys of various kinds with news of happenings in different areas of the country. Not that, until recently, very much worthy of report *had* happened because elves love their quotidian routines and rarely shift from them. Still, Brosista enjoyed the chats and the singing they did together to the accompaniment of the battered old guitar she'd brought back from one of her rare visits to the human zone many moons ago. S/he was particularly partial to the songs of a human called Bobby Zimmerman/

Dylan and taught friends how to sing his words in a language called American. It was all lots of fun.

Then, of course, there were her/his barn animals, with whom s/he conversed in their own tongues and, without whom, she would have found life unendurable. Obviously enough, there were the baby gryphons, hippogriffs, simurghs and chimera who remained babies all their lives but, again taken from a distant human zone visit, she also kept three cats, a chameleon, a toad, a pig, and seventeen rabbits. Brosista was never happier than during the time she spent with them in the barn next to her hut, where they all lived together in slothful peace. Sometimes, they would go off together for walks or hops or swims or flights or whatever, but, mainly, they sat around telling tales of their very disparate backgrounds—and also, occasionally, joining in with the Bobby Zimmerman/Dylan songs.

Life couldn't have been better, especially as the hut and barn were set in a grassy glade on a high slope of Fairyland's only mountain—well actually more like a big hill—from which Brosista commanded a fine view down across the flat lands, valleys, lakes and occasional forest below, whence her/his comrades would bring regular supplies of fruits, vegetables, and other land-grown produce. Elves, it will be remembered, do not eat animals any more than they eat each other. In exchange, Brosista would give them flasks of wine and other potables made from the vineyards s/he maintained, and they would have a party with dancing. Never was money exchanged because nobody had invented it, which was just as well, Brosista considered, given her brief encounters with its evils in the human zone.

There had been a time, back in some yesterday or another, when Fairyland leaders were called "kings" or "queens" depending on the dominant amounts of maleness or femaleness they displayed, but Brosista had done away with all that tosh. Briefly s/he'd toyed with "Kweeng" but that sounded too silly and, so, wishing to stress kinship above inherited regality in the land, had opted for the brother/sister compound s/he reckoned so much more appropriate, and then opened the way for the universal suffrage which had returned her as leader for more yesterdays than s/he could remember. Not, of course, that s/he could remember very many yesterdays, however hard s/he'd tried (see above). Nonetheless, s/he trusted the "family" must have appreciated the abolition of diktats from above, however congenial they may generally have been, and their replacement with a leadership role redefined more as convenor or facilitator, or else she would not have continued to hold the position s/he considered no more important than that of any other fairy. Yes, whenever the moots were held, s/he was the one to sit in the posh chair because *some*one had to keep order or else the occasions would have turned into yet more parties with singing, dancing, joke telling, slippery pole climbing, and dandelion tossing. Mind you, after the moot s/he would join in such revelries with the best of them.

So that was Brosista Oberoni for you, and much loved s/he was by all those with whom s/he came into contact. Until the appearance of the renegade group of populist fascist goblins led by Gobshyte "The Glorious," that was. His mission in life was to persuade Fairylanders to abandon the "lovey dovey bollocks" disseminated by Brosista, in favour of what he termed "self-enterprise," with which message he—yes, a "he" and only a "he"—seemed to be having some alarming success. After so many yesterdays of what he called "blind, mind-numbing obedience to unwritten rules," significant numbers of not only goblins, but also pixies, sprites, leprechauns, boggarts and even brownies amongst others, were calling for "change." To *what*, nobody knew for sure, because Gobshyte himself had no idea beyond the "self-enterprise" slogan, which appeared to mean only "get what's good for you and sod everybody else." Mind you, that was a radical enough suggestion to Fairylanders, especially the young and foolish who had begun attending Gobshyte rallies in their scores and, in some cases, indulging in rapes and pillages. All of which astonished Brosista, who had no idea how to counteract such a menace. It was for this reason, s/he had pleaded with KayCee to come home to help and been delighted at the immediate acceptance of her/his request. Fresh from recent adventures in the human zone, s/he of all fairies would surely have words of wisdom to contribute to the curtailing of these unprecedented and worrisome developments.

"Ah, there you are. How good of you to come. Glass of beansprout brandy, my dear?" s/he'd said as—speak of the elf—into the little hut had materialised a smiling KayCee, who took her/his old friend in a bear hug and said a glass of beansprout brandy would be welcome indeed.

"And possibly a pipe of your special FairyBac for us to share?" s/he added.

"With the greatest of pleasure. By 'special' I assume you mean the one with the..."

"Grass."

Brosista grinned. "Same old KayCee."

~ * ~

Gobshyte, self-dubbed "The Glorious," lived in a cave many fairyfoots (miles) from Brosista's mountain hut. But this was no regular smelly, dank, sort of a cave without mod cons, no siree. Through many yesterdays of his own brand of self-enterprise—mainly theft, trickery, bribery, and in some cases grievous bodily harm—Gobbi, as he liked to be known in populist circles, had turned it into a mini palace dedicated to his own grandeur. Gilt iron gates graced its entrance, behind which an atrium bedecked with framed heroic paintings of himself led off to a much wider chandelier-lit space appointed with specialist amenities—toilets, a grooming alcove, a sleeping space, a lounging area, and a trufflewood desk he had made himself upon which sat the latest model ElfVision transponder computer he used to blazon his messages of populist revolution all across Fairyland. From humble origins Gobbi had indeed come some distance and intended to keep it that way as he travelled the remaining fairyfoots to the highest post in the land. To which end, he had also radically redesigned his appearance. As you will be aware, goblins are not the prettiest of creatures, but the ur-Gobbi had beaten even the most gruesome into a cocked hat such that fellow goblins would turn away and clutch their stomachs should they come across him.

No longer, however. Cosmetic surgery carried out partly by pals who'd visited the human zone, and partly by fourteen yesterdays spent there himself, had ensured a brand new and much more enticing look.

Yes, he was still bandy-legged, stooping, floppy-eared, and hairy in the way necessary to maintaining his street cred amongst other goblins, but the package had been polished into the gritty, yet appealing, image required of any self-respecting revolutionary preparing for a leadership challenge: neatly trimmed and regularly washed face and head hair, creams hiding the wrinkly skin, jeweled rings in the floppy ears, muscles painted into the bow legs, all that type of thing. Plus coaching in not just computer jargon, but also crowd-pulling oration. Yes, this was a Gobshyte who reckoned he was going places and would allow nothing to get in his way. One of his favourite pastimes was strutting up and down in front of the wall length mirror in the grooming alcove spouting such crowd pleasing slogans as "Greedy is Goody," "Brosistaists are losers—lock 'em up," "Fairyland First," "Keep Foreigners Out," "Take Back Control," and of course "Wadda we want?—Change, Change, *CHANGE*. When do we want it? Now, now, *NOW*"—all accompanied by ghoulish grins and meaningful finger pointing at an imaginary crowd.

This was what he was doing when interrupted by his second-in-command, Gobollox, with an urgent message.

"Wadda *you* want?" said Gobshyte in the middle of one of his spurious Keep Foreigners Out rants, spurious because coming from as many backgrounds as they did, *all* fairies were always already foreigners and had never thought anything about it until the populists raised the phantasm. "Can't you see I'm busy?"

"S'cuse me, Your Most Glorious, ever so sorry," said Gobollox. "But there's sunnink you ought to know."

"I already know *every*thing I'll ever need to know, Shit For Brains."

Gobollox blew out his hairy cheeks and investigated a pimple at the end of his nose.

"It's just that…" he ventured.

"*What?*" spluttered Gobshyte at the end of a particularly virulent and prolix passage in which he was comparing foreigners to rancid vermin with smelly bottoms and nasty eating habits who should be exterminated on sight. Against whom he would build a wall right across Fairyland to keep them out of the goblin zone.

"I just thought you'd like to know that KayCee is back."

"Kay...?"

"Cee."

"No I *don't* bloody well see. Now, why don't you just piss off?" Gobshyte was saying. But then, he stopped.

"You mean *that* KayCee? The one who's been fooling around with dirty stinking foreign *humans*?"

Gobollox blew the air out of his cheeks in relief. "The same."

"So? So *what*?"

"Well, news on the grapevine says while s/he was there, s/he disappeared two big time presidents. You've heard of places called America and Russia in the human zone, Your Most Glorious?"

"'Course I have. I know all I need to know, don't I?"

"Indeed, you do," said Gobollox, who knew Gobshyte knew practically nothing about anything and made everything up as he went along, but kept the knowledge to himself. "So you will be aware of the importance of these places in the human power games."

"Of *course* I am."

"Anyway s/he had their presidents disappeared."

Finally getting some of the import of Gobollox's message, Gobshyte curtailed his foreigners' rant and turned around from his mirror.

"Disappeared them *how*?"

"Had them eaten by wild, lower order human zone animals, one a python, the other a woman lion."

Well, that stopped Gobshyte in his tracks, all right. Having no clue what either a python or a woman lion was, and, in truth, knowing nothing at all about human countries called Ameericky or Rushya, as a clever populist/fascist, he nonetheless began to appreciate the significance of Gobollox's interference in his foreigners' rant routine.

"You mean if we could...?" he said, eyes all aglitter

"Exactly, Your Most Glorious." Gobollox preened.

"...Persuade this KayCee across to our side, then s/he might...?"

Gobollox splayed his hairy hands palm upwards, hoisted his hirsute single eyebrow, and finished Gobshyte's question for him.

"Get Brosista eaten, too."

That was when Gobshyte took Gobollox in what he thought of as a fraternal bear hug and said, "Gobo, old fellow, you...are...a...*gen*ius."

Twenty-three

"So KayCee, tell me of your doings in the human zone," said Brosista as the pair passed their FairyBac pipe back and forth. "I've heard rumours, of course, but a fairy can never trust rumours, can s/he? You know how happy our kin are when it comes to making up tall tales."

"Indeed, Brosy. Always fun to suspend one's disbelief for a harmless little fantasy that makes you laugh or think or both, and let oneself be carried along by the 'what-if' ride."

"But when it comes to serious matters..."

"Seek details that verify the story."

"Quite. Which is part of the reason I'm so happy to be talking with you now, my dear. The other part, of course, is what we're going to do about Gobshyte, but *that* may depend on the first part. Do pass the pipe, would you?"

KayCee took a long puff, exhaled with pleasure, handed the pipe over, and gave Brosista a blow-by-blow account of her doings in St Ives, including both the playful naughty bits, and the sudden switch to good fairy with its portentous political outcomes for those in the greatest power positions in the human zone.

"The ones you ate?" said Brosista. "So that tale is true. My dear, I never had you marked as a murdering cannibal," she added, shaking her/his head and tutting significantly.

KayCee nodded. "I thought you might see it that way, and I'm sorry. But let us be clear, shall we? *I* didn't eat them. I had them eaten."

"There's a difference?"

KayCee shrugged. "They were asking for it, and the snake and the lioness I magicked into being were hungry, so I simply allowed nature to take its course. In a sense, one might even argue it was their own greed that caused them to devour them*selves*."

Brosista raised an eyebrow and grinned. "Nice twist of logic. I suppose you *might* see it that way."

"Well, whichever way you see it, the human zone is now a better place—for the moment, in any case. Who knows what other new leaders will emerge and how *they* will screw things up. Humans have a propensity for messing their own beds, as you well know."

Brosista nodded sadly. "Indeed. One wonders when they will ever learn. There's little evidence of it so far. And how long have they been going now?"

"In various forms, a few million of what they call 'years.' During which they've invented more and worse machines to help destroy themselves and their environment."

"And on they go squabbling and fighting, too."

"Even though all their various gods tell them they shouldn't."

"Must be a pretty dispiriting job being a human god. Jolly glad *we* don't need them. Anyway, *any*way, let us turn to matters back home, shall we? Not exactly as if fairies are behaving *all* that well, at the moment. One fears there may have been some adverse influence from the human zone, too many signals picked up from there, perhaps?"

"Very possibly. Too much tourist traffic, so too much exposure to the mayhem and madness."

"Which may well be where yucky Gobshyte learnt his terrible trade. What *are* we to do about him and his gang, KayCee? I do hope you have some bright ideas. Which do *not* include having them eaten, however barbarically they are behaving. As you know, we do not tolerate killing for any reason."

KayCee smiled. "I wouldn't dream of it, Brosy. The magic that worked on humans would not work here, anyhow. Fairies are too canny to fall for their very own types of trickery, and goblin though he may be, Gobshyte is no fool."

"Quite. So, any other ideas?" said Brosista, passing back the FairyBac pipe at which KayCee drew hard before exhaling thoughtfully.

"Well, I have had *one.*"

"Do tell."

"It may sound a mite implausible and, do please say so if that is what you think, but I just wonder if, having done them a service or two, a couple of my favourite humans might be prepared to reciprocate."

Brosista arched her other eyebrow. *Humans?* How?"

"By my inviting them over here for a brief visit."

"*Here?* To Fairyland? They wouldn't speak any of our languages, they would stand out like sore wings, and worse still, they would be foreigners. You know how much play Gobshyte has made with *for*eigners even though there aren't any."

"Yes, yes, I understand. But I could always interpret and translate at the mass meetings."

"Mass meetings?"

"Gobshyte's. The ones we would infiltrate with our tame, friendly, and beneficent human foreigners in the same way, so I hear, that he has plagued Brosistaite gatherings across the land with his *agents provocateurs*, but this time there would be none of their violence, harassment and threats. The very antithesis, in fact."

Brosista smiled as s/he digested the idea. "To make our folk see what fools they've been to swallow Gobshyte's xenophobic nonsense," she said. "Worth a try, I suppose. And you have some tame, friendly, and beneficent humans in mind for this job? They'd have to be pretty unusual—*and* brave."

KayCee grinned. "Let me think on it. But yes, there are a couple of candidates who fit the bill and might be so persuaded.

~ * ~

Gobshyte wasted no time upping the ante in his campaign to, "wipe the scourge of Brosista," from Fairyland's fair land. The very next tomorrow after finding out from Gobollox about KayCee's return, he blasted the homegrown version of Twitter (Tooter) with a succession of vitriolic toots claiming Brosista to be a "puppet of foreigner agents," "a perverter of Fairyland values," a "hoarder of ill-gotten gains," "a whore," a "smelly bottom," and "a changeling" who deserved to be locked up pending the trial which would surely find her guilty and hand down the death penalty. To whet appetites yet further, he also suggested a peculiarly gruesome form of punishment; being eaten alive by a specially magicked gryphon. "NO OTHER FORM OF PUNISHMENT WOULD BE EQUAL TO HER/HIS CRIMES AGAINST FAIRIES," he concluded, adding he knew the very elf who could see to it the job was done properly, having just returned from the human zone where s/he'd engineered the same retribution on equally bad humans. No names mentioned, but the reference was clear to those who kept pace with local news. As was the inference s/he was in Gobshyte's pocket.

(N.B. All Gobshyte's messages have been translated from their original Goblinese with corrections of all syntactical and lexical errata, of which there was one in every second word of the original).

The reaction to this outburst was not immediate but more of a slow burn. Fairies aren't fools. Not in all the years of Brosista's peaceful "reign" had they needed to put their heads above any parapets, fearing that way only danger and disruption lay. Better by far to keep one's own counsel on matters political and voice their opinions only to close friends. Yes, increasing numbers had turned out for Gobshyte's rallies, but many of them only for the spectacle, and a bit of a laugh at the finger-pointing pantomime artist claiming to become their next leader.

"Yeah, yeah, fat chance," was the most frequent response in grassy glade gatherings following such events. "My arse has more chance of getting the top job than that bozo. Another drop of the burdock brandy?" After which, the topic would be forgotten until the next rally.

That is not to say, however, that *nobody* took Gobshyte's outbursts seriously (see above somewhere). There was a disturbing minority of young, poor, and uneducated folk—mainly of goblin, troll, or boggart ancestry—who saw Gobshyte as the only true messiah and felt emboldened by his outrageous speeches to become outrageous themselves, hence the raping and pillaging. But even more concerning than these blatant rejections of fairy lore was the insidious manner in which these renegades began speaking ill of others, especially elves, equating them to foreigners and claiming they had no right to continue living in Fairyland. Such were the seeds of revolt Gobshyte had sewn and, piano piano, the seeds had begun to sprout. With this latest bout of bombast, however, they had taken to blossoming to such an extent that even the safety-first naysayers of yesterday had to sit up and take heed. As noted, there was no immediate impact but, through hints and whispers in clandestine meetings across the land—each of them attended and stirred by populist/fascist agents—the burn showed distinct signs of turning from slow to at least a healthy crackle of fire. After all, even the erstwhile sensible and peaceable fairies didn't want to be on the losing side, did they? And within fourteen or fifteen tomorrows, the Tootiesphere began to burgeon with toots of approval for Gobshyte's words.

"The Glorious" was delighted but, sitting together before their ElfVision screen, Brosista and KayCee were far from it, particularly KayCee, given the none too oblique reference to her human zone exploits. "He even *mentions* me again, he does so at his peril," s/he declared.

"Divide and rule, eh? That's his plan," said Brosista. "Where there was peace, create chaos and hope to win."

"Through mere words, slogans with no verification."

"Lies and bogus promises of a better Fairyland. Even Cyndy can see through that crap," said Brosista, stroking the head of her Italian Greyhound who, in her estimation, was the finest creature ever to have come from the human zone. "Can't you, darling?"

Cyndy said nothing beyond a mild groan, because Italian Greyhounds aren't big speakers. But from the look she gave Brosista with her amber eyes and the accompanying tail wag, it was clear she was in full agreement with her master/mistress, who went on to say,

"And I shall not countenance similar tactics in my defence, for that would demean us all."

"And prove counter-productive," said KayCee, "because that's precisely what Gobshyte *wants* you to do. There's nothing he'd like better than to draw you into a battle of mud-slinging he knows he would win. Such a person has no conscience and recognizes no boundaries. In the human zone, he would be termed a psychopath."

"Which is?" said Brosista, who had no concept of such a creature.

"You want a full definition?"

"Please."

"Someone who displays pathological lying, a grandiose sense of self, cunning and manipulation, lack of remorse or guilt, callousness and lack of empathy, sexual promiscuity, a lack of realistic long-term goals, impulsivity, failure to accept responsibility, short-term marital relationships, and criminal versatility."

"Goodness me, that's some list. *How* could you possibly remember all that lot?"

"It's the kind of memory I have, which can be a damn nuisance, because I can't forget *any*thing. Mind cluttered with so many trivia they can get in the way of proper thinking."

"As opposed to mine." Brosista sighed. "Which sometimes can't even remember its own name. Anyway, *any*way, that pretty well sums up Gobshyte. What was the word for him again...a sicko what?"

"Path. Psychopath."

"Must try to remember that, but you can bet your life it'll be gone by tomorrow. So, KayCee, d'you reckon that's the sort of description your tame humans might use when they come over to help us out? Far be it from me, as you might imagine."

"No they won't, because that, too, would be another own goal against us. But they will know well enough the type of individual we're dealing with because the term describes both the creeps I removed for the sake of at least the *possibility* of peace in the human zone. No, I shall counsel them to avoid any such overt reference, because fairies wouldn't understand it anyway."

"So what *will* they do?"

"Behave antithetically to deconstruct the bastard."

"Pardon?"

"Demonstrate the plausibility and benefits of the polar opposite of such behaviour."

"The kind Fairyland has always known."

"Exactly, but with the extra advantage of coming from the lips of the very 'foreigners' Gobshyte has devoted so much time to vilifying."

Brosista smiled. "From the mouths of devils shall come words of wisdom."

"The ones I have in mind may need a little coaching, but yes, that's the general idea."

Brosista toked hard on the FairyBac pipe and shook her/his head in perplexity. "It's a long shot…"

"But the best one we have on the table at the moment. Unless you have any better ideas."

"Truth be told, my dear, I'm not as young as I used to be. It's a long time since I had what you might call an idea. There will come a tomorrow when a younger elf will need to replace me. You possibly…?"

KayCee took her old mentor in a close embrace, told him/her not to think such thoughts, and said s/he had no ambitions whatsoever in that direction.

"Let us just take one step at a time to solve the problem in hand. With which, I'm sure, Cyndy here would agree. Wouldn't you, Cyndy?"

One of the many peculiar attributes of Italian Greyhounds when pleased is they are able to smile. Lift their lips, show their teeth, and smile. Which is what Cyndy did.

"Well that seals it," said Brosista, taking the tiny dog in her arms and sitting her upright on her knees so she looked the spit of a meerkat. "Cyndy's advice I never ignore, do I sweetheart?"

In a rare moment of vocalisation, Cyndy purred not unlike a contented cat. "Prrrrr," she went in a long sigh, then closed her amber eyes.

Twenty-four

When KayCee materialised translucently into forty-eight Salubrious Street, the family—William, Stephanie, Ernest, Georgina, James and Gabi—were sitting around a newly acquired fifth-hand upright piano on which Norbert was belting out rickety versions of Little Richard and Jerry Lee Lewis songs. As s/he floated down into their midst, he was jumping up and down before the instrument warbling the prepositionally flawed line, "Goodness *gracious* great balls *on* fire," causing the children to giggle and the others to smirk awkwardly.

"I thought he'd been a bloody Stasi officer. What's he doing playing *this* stuff?" James whispered to Gabi, who shook her head.

"A man of many talents, I guess. After the wall came down, the old East suddenly got all kinds of American music. Some said it was brainwashing, but nobody cared about that. After all those years of military marches, they just let it all hang out. It was only rock 'n' roll but..."

James smiled as Norbert launched into "Good Golly Miss Molly." "They liked it."

"Loved it. Especially, once they'd heard The Stones and The Beatles," Gabi was saying, as through some sixth sense Norbert abruptly canned Little Richard and strummed out the opening chords to "Hey Jude," at which William began going "nah, nah, nah, nah-nuh-nah-nah" and inviting everybody to get up and dance. Which wasn't an easy operation given the tiny size of twenty-eight Salubrious Street's parlour, but up they all jumped and, joining arms, took to swaying about as Norbert sang about taking sad songs and making them better. KayCee smiled and, casting aside the translucency in favour of the old Koleen persona, joined in.

For a moment in the general jollity, nobody noticed, but then, James became aware it was no longer Gabi to whom he was connected but a small person with an elf's head and Marilyn Monroe legs.

"Koleen? Holy shit," he said peering down. "What're *you* doing here?"

"Tell you when the song's over. I like this one. And from now on, I'm KayCee, okay?" said the elf as Norbert warbled about how it was only fools who played it cool and made their worlds a little colder.

And pretty soon they were back to the nah, nah, nahing at which Norbert left the piano to its own devices and took to waving his arms about as he conducted the longest chorus in pop history. It was only then that he, too, recognised KayCee and acknowledged her/his presence with the familiar salute that drew Gabi's attention to the new presence in their midst.

"What...the...?" she said, standing stock still and goggle eyed.

That's when Norbert hastily quit his burgeoning musical career, hurried over to throw an arm around his favourite long-lost cousin's shoulders and whispered in her ear, "You remember the elf you didn't believe in when we told you?"

Gabi nodded distractedly. "And wuh-what's it duh-doing huh-*here* now?"

"Not an 'it,' both a he and a she," Norbert corrected, reminding Gabi of the genderless nature of KayCee's part of Fairyland. "As to why s/he's here I don't know. Possibly just a little visit to check everything's A-Okay. Why don't we go over and ask?"

"Uh-okay. You're shuh-sure it's safe for the children?"

"Look for yourself," said Norbert, pointing over at Ernest and Georgina who were enfolded in the embrace KayCee had grown a metre to offer.

"Auntie Gabi, didn't I *tell* you fairies were for real?" said Ernest. "And friendly. Come and see for yourself."

It was James who took Gabi by the hand and took her across to meet the being, who—although James didn't know it—had contributed to her pregnancy and accelerated it by several weeks.

"KayCee, say hello to my wife," he said.

Gabi chewed her lower lip and said the ambiguous thing parents say when introduced to their child's new best friend: "Hello, I've heard a lot about you."

"All good, I hope," KayCee replied with a wink. "And yes, I *am* an elf. You'll get over it, all the others have," s/he added, wafting an arm at the present company. "Ain't that so, folks?"

William, Stephanie, James, and Norbert nodded.

"Wanna see me do one of my tricks?"

"Yessss," Ernest and Georgina chorused, defying the adults to disagree.

"Okay, then. The honour of choosing goes to the children. Who would you like me to turn into, kids?"

Ernest and Georgina conflabbed and decided on a hobbit, but KayCee pouted and winced a bit at that suggestion.

"Aw, couldn't you come up with something harder? Hobbits are too easy peasy."

Ernest frowned. Georgina scratched her head. "Um...erm..." they said until Georgina ventured, "Santa Claus?"

But KayCee didn't fancy that either, reckoning it too commonplace. "I tell you what though, how about Rudolf?"

"Nureyev?" said William, performing what he thought of as a *pas de deux*.

But KayCee had Santa's red-nosed friend in mind and, after muttering the magic words extropool/looportxe and clicking his/her fingers a few times, there before the family stood a fully-antlered albeit miniature reindeer.

"Hi there, folks," it said in a Mid-Western, American accent. "Anybody wanna ride?"

Which Ernest and Georgina surely did. Playing Nelly the elephant with their dad was one thing, but climbing aboard Santa's favourite reindeer quite another. And to complete the experience, Norbert hurried back to the piano and produced a wonky, but recognizable, version of "Rudolf the Red-Nosed Reindeer" along with some muddled lyrics about how all the other reindeers called him names and wouldn't let him join in reindeer games. It wasn't Yuletide, but it might as well have been. Finally persuaded, even Gabi joined in the fun, slapping Rudolf on the bottom, laughing, and shouting "Giddy up there, Rudi."

At which, for the terrifying second in which KayCee muttered the magic reversal words looportxe/extropool, s/he, Ernest and Georgina dematerialized and were nowhere to be seen.

"Aaaaaaaghhhh," Gabi was on the cusp of screaming but choked back her angst the very next second when the chuckling elf and giggling children were back amongst them.

"Wow, some fun," said Ernest. "Didn't I *tell* you to believe in fairies?"

KayCee bowed and smiled as Norbert returned from his piano and said, "But surely you didn't drop by just to show off your party pieces."

"Indeed not, *Herr* Kriegskraft," said a newly serious KayCee. "I wonder if I could tempt you, James, and Gabi to the pub down the road for a little chat? Sorry to break up the family gathering, but I have a proposition for you.

~ * ~

In Fairyland, through a broadside of barely legible toots and occasional personal appearances, Gobshyte was upping even more ante. Not content with slandering Brosista, he went on to outline a new vision for what he termed "his people"—the poor, the disaffected, those left behind by lassie fare (sic) economicalists in the government "swamp"—for whom he intended building a paradise homeland with the promised giant wall to separate them from the rest of Fairyland. There, in Gobshyteland, they would live a life of prosperity and perpetual bliss unaffected by the machinations of the "criminal smelly-bottoms" currently running the country, who would systematically be disenfranchised, hunted down wherever they might try to hide, and eaten raw.

"No more of their rapin' an' a'pillagin'," he screamed at his worryingly larger audiences, conveniently forgetting it was *his* followers, at *his* invitation, who had been responsible for all the recorded raping and pillaging to date.

Whoops and cheers from the (mostly drunken) crowds he addressed. Hats thrown in the air, that type of thing as he strutted up and down before them jabbing admonitory fingers in the direction of Brosista's hilltop hut many fairyfoots away.

"No more of their snot-nosed, hoity toity, clever pants hypocritizer (sic) schmooze. Peace and love and all that crap. No siree. You *can* always git what you want."

More hat-throwing, plus explosions from some homemade fireworks.

"An' no more kowtowin' to freakin' foreigners. You know how you can tell a foreigner?" he would confide leaning down towards his admirers.

"No, *NO*, tell us, Gobbi."

"'Cos they don't look like us, that's how. Different lingo, different colour, smelly bottoms...and *they're* the ones who've been stealin' all our goods at the dead of night when we're asleep an' not payin' attention."

"Ass's holes, forest freaks, lowlife lumpbums," would come the response scripted by Gobollox and his cronies who would be mingling in the crowd ready to scrotum squeeze anybody not heard screaming such insults.

"Right, *right, DAMN RIGHT.* Well, lemme...tell...you...good folks, *NO MORE.* You meet one around the place, you just knock it right down. From here on in, the message is Gobshyteland First and go screw the rest. Lemme hear you say it."

Roars of "Gobshyteland First and go screw the rest" from the crowd, some of the roars a little squeaky because of the scrotum squeezing, but Gobshyte didn't care about that, just paced up and down his podium nodding approval—of the response, but mainly of himself for being such a magnetic and popular candidate. When back home in his luxury cave, he would manipulate and magnify the attendance numbers at such rallies, and then toot them across the whole of Fairyland, claiming to be the best and most popular potential leader it had ever known in the whole of its yesterdays. Also the prettiest, savviest, fiercest, cuddliest...but then he ran out of superlatives.

~ * ~

At the Fox and Ferret hostelry, KayCee, in male local yokel garb of blue jeans and a fisherman's pullover, bought pints of Cornish Special Pale Ale for him/herself, Norbert and James, and a spritzer for Gabi before the quartet sat themselves down in a quiet corner of the lounge bar. Along the way, s/he'd apologized for dragging them from the party but hoped they'd understand s/he wouldn't have done so had the situation not been a little urgent.

"Trouble on the home front," s/he'd explained as they ambled along.

"Home being...?" Norbert asked.

"*My* home. Fairyland."

"What sort of trouble?" said Gabi, who had come to not only accept, but like, KayCee once her initial qualms had been put to rest.

"I'll explain when we get to the pub."

"And you've come back here to escape them," said James. "Good plan."

Norbert frowned at this unreflective conclusion. There was little that passed under his radar where his favourite elf was concerned, and in his experience, s/he wasn't the sort to run away from trouble. Far from it, *vide* matters back in Berlin and more recently in St Ives. KayCee had something up her sleeve, no question about it. And that something had to do with him, James, and Gabi.

"Care to explain?" he asked but s/he wouldn't be drawn until they were settled in the pub.

"Then I'll tell you," s/he said. "Also there's a video I'd like you to see."

And s/he was true to her word. It wasn't until they'd all sipped at their drinks and nodded appreciatively, that KayCee bit the bullet s/he, even *s/he*, had been anticipating with some trepidation. After all, asking three humans to agree to be shrunk to elf size—albeit maintaining their human form—and then be teleported to Fairyland to confront and overturn the doings of a crazed goblin was a big ask.

It was Norbert who helped her out. "Perhaps before we hear why it is to us you've turned," he said, "you'd like to show us the video you mentioned. It might help us understand the 'troubles' you spoke of."

"Okay. Thanks. Yes, perhaps it would," KayCee replied, checking there were no other customers looking over their shoulders. There weren't, but it wouldn't have mattered if there had been. Images of a Gobshyte rally would have struck them as no more than some sort of new computer game.

So it was that KayCee extracted from a satchel a mini laptop and, with a running translation of Gobshyte's words, gave Norbert, Gabi, and James a taste of the kind of troubles she'd mentioned. It ran for maybe five minutes, at the end of which Norbert said, "That bastard sounds just like Dougal Klank. You're sure it's not him come back to life as a goblin?"

KayCee grinned. "No chance. But you're right, the ideas are every bit as obnoxious, and somehow or another, we need to eradicate them from Fairyland before they have a chance to take root."

"*We?*" said James.

KayCee twiddled his/her thumbs, shrugged, twiddled the thumbs some more, raised two optimistic eyebrows, and whispered, "Well, I was rather wondering whether you guys might help out a little."

"From *here?*" said Gabi. "I don't quite see how we could..."

It was yet again super-radar Norbert who came to the rescue. "You would like us to come back with you, wouldn't you?"

Going for broke, KayCee nodded. "I know it's an awful lot to hope for, and you must please feel free to say no, but you're right, Norbert. You'd be entirely safe, I promise, and it would only be for a very short time. It's just occurred to me that the best way to puncture

Gobshyte's balloon would be to show Fairylanders foreigners are *not* their enemies."

There followed a hiatus as Norbert, James, and Gabi digested this bizarre request. After all, it's not every day of the week a person gets asked to go to Fairyland, let alone to stem an insurrection. All manner of questions posed themselves. Why them and not William or Stephanie, for example? How would they travel and in what form? Given the disparity in sizes between fairies and humans, they would stick out like elephants in rooms, which would be *frightening* and thus counterproductive for KayCee's friendly foreigner plan. What *was* the plan anyway? Those were just some of the uncertainties buzzing through the minds KayCee read without much difficulty, although s/he was pleased also to note that none of the trio doubted their debt to him/her for the job s/he'd done in the human zone. Willingness to return the kindness was there in spades, but we weren't talking an overnighter in Los Angeles or even a trip in a space shuttle, were we? What we were talking was a visit to a zone in which nobody believed except children and loonies.

Without waiting for those doubts to be voiced, KayCee answered them with understanding and humility. Of course she sympathized with their concerns but:

1) William and Stephanie couldn't go because they needed to stay home and mend their family.

2) Norbert, Gabi, and James would travel at elf height, but in human form, and be teleported at three times the speed of light.

3) The plan was still embryonic in her mind but, in essence, would expose renegade fairies to the obverse of the fears Gobshyte was fuelling in the guise of three nice humans.

Then s/he thanked them for their recognition of the job s/he'd done in St Ives and assured them s/he appreciated their desire to reciprocate.

It was Norbert who responded with thanks to KayCee and a tentative willingness to participate before pointing out that:

1) Not all humans *were* nice, so the appearance of himself, for example, who had once been very nasty, might be cheating a bit,

mightn't it? No such aspersions would he cast James's or Gabi's way but...

And,

2) How could the appearance of a mere three humans, however nicely they behaved, possibly counteract the venom they had just witnessed in the Gobshyte video?

KayCee nodded, having foreseen such objections, and fielded them easily enough.

"In answer to your first point," s/he said. "I have to agree, of course, I do. But having once been somewhat nasty in the past gives you a unique and helpful insight into the condition and how it might be countered. Not so? After all, you're not such a bad fellow now, are you?"

Norbert smiled and nodded. "I guess not."

"And in any case, it's not absolutes we're talking here. No-one is absolutely nice, not even *me*." KayCee giggled. "You will remember some of my little tricks well enough. But, and this is an important qualification, we can always pretend, can't we? A spot of theatricality never did anybody any harm, and that's what you'd be doing. Putting on a show. What we're talking here is a metaphor, a memorable image, the sorts of thing your advertising industry uses to stimulate the subliminal desire to buy."

"Lies, therefore," said James.

"Quite, but all in a good cause, I'm sure you'll agree." KayCee smiled. "And on Norbert's second point, it doesn't really matter how *many* humans turn up as long as their repartee is consistent and widely disseminated. You must remember there is one crucial difference between the fairy and human zones when it comes to bedrock thought."

"Which is?" asked Gabi.

"That your Dougal Klank and Igor Ripurpantzov were only the latest in a long historical line of the autocratic narcissists you guys have been exposed to for centuries. They're in your blood. Okay, we removed those two, but others will follow on the swings and roundabouts of your governance. In Fairyland, by contrast, Gobshyte is the *first* of his kind. There are *no* precedents for his sort of behaviour and in any case, fairies have very short memories."

"Which would make the handling of the situation more plausible," Norbert concluded. "Like a successful cancer operation."

"Exactly, and, thank you, Norbert. A case of a focused one-off incision and bingo."

And so it was, after a brief conflab, that Norbert, Gabi, and James agreed to join only a tiny select handful of humans ever truly to have visited Fairyland.

"Do we go right now, immediately?" said Gabi.

"Tch, tch, no," KayCee replied. "First we must discuss the nature of my plan, which will need some elaboration and to be agreed with Brosista, my boss. And, of course, your absence will need to be explained to William, Stephanie, Ernest and Georgina."

"We'll just tell them we're going back to London," said James. "After all, there's no particular reason for us to stay in St Ives any longer now matters have returned to normal."

"My thinking exactly. Another round of libations to toast the success of our little adventure?" said KayCee, rising from his/her chair. "On me, of course, in eternal gratitude for your generosity of mind and spirit."

"Thanks but not for me." Gabi chuckled, patting her growing tummy. "Eat for two, yes. But not drink for two."

Norbert and James had no such reservations, however and, by the time they'd bought another round each, were just a tad tipsy by the time they returned to number forty-eight Salubrious Place.

Twenty-five

It was two days later in human time that KayCee, Gabi, James, and Norbert materialised together in the ramshackle barn Brosista kept for both her animals and the occasional overnight guest. Not the most luxurious of accommodations, but it had never occurred to Brosista that animals and fairies should occupy different living spaces. They all breathed the air, and walked, flew or swam the same land, skies or waters, so why treat them separately was his/her thinking. The only exception s/he made was for Cyndy, the Italian Greyhound, who had her own snuggle bed in the hut, although, she preferred to creep under Brosista's blankets at night and Brosista had given up trying to stop her.

"Gosh," chorused the tiny miniature versions of Norbert, James and Gabi as they gazed at the menagerie of baby gryphons, hippogriffs, simurghs, chimera, three cats, a chameleon, a toad, a pig and seventeen rabbits, who produced a cacophony of animal noises at the sight of their new guests.

"My little family," said Brosista in passable English. "I'm sure they'll make you *very* welcome. And thank you sooo much for popping over to help out."

"This is where we'll be...?" said Gabi

"Sleeping, yes," said KayCee.

"But you will, of course, be eating in my hut with me," Brosista clarified. "And you will not be sleeping along*side* my friends, although I'm sure they'd be very welcoming. No, no, if you would just take a look to your left, you'll see a ladder taking you up to nice little platform on which I have laid out four rather pretty palliasses with pillows and hand woven blankets for your super comfort."

"Great, fantastic," said Norbert on behalf of the group, although neither James nor Gabi looked particularly impressed until reassured by a whisper from KayCee that none of the animals was allowed up there and, from personal experience, she could guarantee the beds were specially designed to the highest fairy standards to guarantee what s/he termed "a magical night's repose."

"You'll be sleeping up there, too?" asked Gabi.

"Indeed, I shall. From here on in, you guys are my priority at all times."

"And young KayCee here is the finest chaperone a person could wish for, trust me," said Brosista, having mind read the Cockburns' concerns. "So, having seen your quarters, should we perhaps relocate to my little hut where refreshments await and you can be introduced to my housemate, Cyndy? Follow me do."

"Housemate?" Norbert said sotto voce to KayCee. "A sister perhaps? A significant other?"

KayCee smiled. "You'll see when we get there."

And sure enough they did when Cyndy, waiting behind the hut's front door, went into her specialist Italian Greyhound repertoire of balletic twirls on her hind legs with the front ones pawing air before resting them on the shoulders of each new arrival and giving them a kiss. Which wasn't hard, seeing as Norbert, James and Gabi were small enough for an IG to reach them with ease. It was all very heartwarming.

~ * ~

Brosista, KayCee, Cyndy, Gabi, James and Norbert spent the next four tomorrows taking convivial saunters around the countryside surrounding Brosista's hut. Down the hillside, they went to explore more grassy glades, farm lands, rivulets and little lakes, stopping along the way to greet villagers who showed far less surprise than Norbert and company expected when they were introduced. Like Brosista and KayCee, they too were given herbal teas and biscuits to consume and asked after their health with little more than a raised eyebrow.

"Did you tell them we were coming?" James asked after one such encounter.

"And we were humans," Norbert added.

KayCee laughed. "No need. As you will begin to understand, fairies at peace are polite, hospitable and trusting folk willing to bend their minds to all sorts of oddities. It's in the tradition. They'll gossip and speculate after you've left them, of course, they will, but that's about the size of it."

Gabi laughed along. "And *we* are now the oddities. That makes a change."

"A nice one, I hope," said Brosista.

"Indeed," said Norbert, whose life had been spent as an outsider and, usually, a pretty problematic one at that. "But given such inborn kindness, *how* can they have fallen for Gobshyte's machinations?"

KayCee winced and shrugged. "Human zone influence possibly. I have no single explanation, although some of my brothers and sisters can, at times, be tragically childlike."

"And his ideas? You reckon they came from us humans, too?" James asked.

"Who knows? They came out of a clear blue sky like an evil wind."

"And, we hope, can be returned whither they came with no more puff inside it," said Brosista as they left one tiny village constructed of wattle and daub shacks. "Speaking of which, have you guys come up with any plans for achieving that, yet?"

Norbert, Gabi and William shook their heads and turned to KayCee for an answer. They'd batted around several ideas with her/him at bedtimes, but so far there was no clear way forward. What could *not* be done—like emulating *any* of Gobshyte's tactics—had been explained at length, but even s/he had been at a loss when it came to how exactly her human allies could be deployed to demonstrate their friendship and counter the new fear of foreigners threatening the traditional peace. Now, as they sat together in a grassy glade with its own rivulet, all but Gabi puffing at a shared pipe of FairyBac, s/he announced the fragment of an idea that had struck her in a dream the previous night.

"It might sound silly," s/he said, "but…"

"C'mon, out with it. We're ready to give anything a shot," said Norbert.

"Laughter," s/he said.

Brosista, Norbert, Gabi and James exchanged puzzled looks.

"Care to elaborate?" said Brosista, passing the pipe to James. "I've yet to witness anything funny about current events in the goblin zone."

"Precisely my point," said KayCee, stroking Cyndy, who had sprung onto her lap wanting a snuggle. "Let me ask you all a question, okay?"

"Okay," her companions chorused.

"What would a self-obsessed, psychopath such as Gobshyte, be least likely to tolerate?"

A number of possibilities floated through people's heads: being branded a loser, ignored, or *called* a self-obsessed psychopath in public inter alia. But then, James had it.

"Being laughed at," he said. "Psychos don't have a sense of humour, especially not when it's directed against them. They may not under*stand* what's going on or why, but they certainly wouldn't tolerate it for long."

"Bingo, go to the top of the class," said KayCee, at which James climbed a little tree and bowed thespianly.

"But fairies do," said Brosista. "There's nothing they like better than a good chuckle, even if they're the butt of it. All taken in the best of spirits."

"A capacity shared by some humans, vide young James up there," said KayCee. "In some parts of the human zone, having what they call "the piss" taken out of them by friends is a key factor in social networking and, indeed, is the hallmark of what they call 'clowns' and 'comedians,' who *make* themselves look foolish precisely to generate laughs.

Brosista looked at Norbert, Gabi, and James—up his tree—and grinned. "I see, KayCee. Good thinking, but I still don't see how this will work out in practice."

"I'm still thinking about that. Watch this space, Brosy."

~ * ~

All that night while the others slept the sleep of the just, KayCee did precisely what she'd promised; thought about it. And while doing so, came across problem after problem. Okay, so laughter could be a key element in any strategy in order both to counter Gobshyte's xenophobia and draw upon fairies' innate playfulness. The question, as Brosista had noted, was how. Initial thoughts included visits to villages across the land by Norbert, Gabi, and James, who would play funny games, dress up in comic costumes, and join in fairy dances at which they would make fools of themselves by failing horribly at the steps, but not minding, and just laughing at their own clumsiness. Then, they could also be infiltrated into Gobshyte rallies to tell jokes and tickle fairies with special tickling sticks such that they drew attention away from the madman on the podium. And s/he also dreamed up an ElfVision comedy series in which the trio acted out sketches based on some of KayCee's favourites from the human zone, such as Laurel and Hardy, Charlie Chaplin, The Marx Brothers and Buster Keaton, which relied less on language and more on visual slapstick.

These were all fun and achievable mind-changing concepts, but probably only sideshow factors given the immensity of the challenge s/he faced from Gobshyte, who was the one at whom the laughter had to be directed, the one to be lampooned to within an inch of his life. And if, as s/he suspected, he *had* picked up at least some of his populist trickery from contact with the human zone through one means or another, he may even have learnt the art of turning a blind eye and a deaf ear to mockery. After all, although KayCee had visited the zone in person more than most, leaks to the less experienced would always continue and, gruesome though they were, Gobshyte and Gobollox were no fools. It wouldn't have taken much for them to learn from the loathsome, yet apparently successful, tactics of the likes of not only the leaders of USA and Russia but also hard-nosed liars and cheats of a similar populist ilk all across the lands of what was called Europe. For an awful moment, and despite the wails of protest that would come from Brosista, KayCee even contemplated using her methods of disposing of Klank and Ripurpantzov on Gobshyte and Gobollox… but stopped herself just in time. After all, a murdered folk hero can become a myth, and a legend able to generate even more followers than the original. A short breathing space in their absence, but then a mass return to their evil ways—which, on reflection, KayCee also feared for the human zone, despite her best endeavours. So *that* was a big no-no. Whichever plan was to be developed would have to contain no violence or emulation of Gobshyte's brutality and give him *no* room to claim victories in the face of transparent defeats. That was a game he knew only too well as a psycho who had no idea of failure, no code of ethics, would lie through his teeth without remorse and turn any competitor into a beatable foe. Instead, he must be made to project an image *so* absurd that even he would be forced to bow to its reality. Whatever s/he devised would have to be without conceptual precedent in either the human or fairy zones and come from way out in left field. And that was one *big* problem for anybody, even the gifted KayCee, who tossed and turned, turned and tossed on her/his special fairy palliasse. No "magical night's repose" for KayCee on this portentous night.

Until there came a voice from the other side of their barn platform, that was. "You okay over there? Need a little chat perhaps?" It was Gabi.

"Mmmm."

"I'll be right over."

"Thanks."

And when Gabi asked what the matter was, KayCee told her in some detail of her struggles to formulate a workable plan of action and was pleased Gabi, at least, warmed to the peripheral roles she, James and Norbert might play.

"But those can't be the *only* strategies. There's still something missing," KayCee said.

"And that is?"

"Quite *how* we capitalize on the laughter idea when it comes to Gobshyte. It's one thing to show fairies the funny side of humans so they needn't fear such strangers any longer, but somehow we must also make Gobshyte and his cronies *look* ridiculous such that they will lose all credibility and never again be taken seriously."

"Mmm. A tricky one," Gabi mused.

"If we could achieve just that, we would be well on the way to victory. As you know, fairies have short memories and, given sufficient ongoing reinforcement will soon forget populism ever even existed, let alone that they took part in it."

"Mmm," Gabi repeated.

"Sorry to burden you with this but it's been going around my head all night, and the answer just will not come. I know it's my responsibility. I'm the one who asked you guys over here, I'm the one who knows the territory, and I'm the one who must make the decisions, but..."

"Many times in my life I have faced similar difficulties," said Gabi. "And I know how hard it can be. When you have a problem that looks insoluble because there are too many trees for you to see the wood."

"Precisely."

"I have one little suggestion, though. It may sound silly and, please, feel free to say so. After all, I am a mere human, but..."

KayCee smiled. "Fire away, woman. Not *all* humans are crazy, and any idea would be gratefully received."

Which was when Gabi cleared her throat and told of a fiction she'd once read in which objectionable politicians in the UK and America had been given their comeuppance by a friendly elf who had turned their bodies into those of infamous fools and seen them laughed out of town.

"Obviously, we couldn't do *that* because, as I understand it, fairies are used to metamorphoses of all sorts and wouldn't necessarily pay any attention."

"Quite so."

"And human examples would have no resonance in Fairyland, anyway."

KayCee nodded.

"But what if we—*you* because it would be your magic needed to play the trick—were to tamper with the language that Gobshyte and Gobollox spout such that it sounds like gobbledygook?"

KayCee laughed. "*Gob*bledygook eh? I like the association. What does it mean?"

"Nonsense, gibberish, phooey, hogwash, balderdash, drivel…" said Gabi, who had run a special seminar in Heidelberg for English slang and jargon.

"Or even bollocks?"

"Indeed. And if we—you—were to fine tune the magic, along with the bollocks, we might get them saying not only unintelligible things, but the precise opposite of what they were intending to say."

"Which could work with their toots as well as their mouths," said KayCee, warming to the idea.

"You think *that* might make Fairyland chuckle? Especially if Norbert, James and I prepared the ground with some little foolishnesses of our own?"

"Chuckle it would make us, no question. Even more if I fiddled with their features just a tad. Miss Human, you are a genius. Would you mind if I were to give you a hug?"

"It would give me the greatest pleasure," said Gabi, the one-time fairy sceptic through whose head were already running examples of the language games they could play, spoonerisms and malapropisms inter alia. "And Norbert, James, and I would be only too happy to mingle with the crowds at Gobshyte rallies and focus the laughter," she added when the hugging was over. "Making absolutely sure it was directed at the bad guys. And you don't think such manipulation would be too hard for you to achieve?"

"Never done it before, babe, but there's always a first time for everything. Just leave it with me. Now, look it's late and, if you'd forgive me I should…"

"Get some sleep. Me, too."

And so it was that KayCee finally did get her magical night's repose, albeit somewhat curtailed. But that still left time for a couple of dreams that had her giggling when s/he awoke.

Twenty-six

In the first of KayCee's dreams, Gobshyte gatecrashes a goblin and boggart music festival, leaps onto the stage dressed as a phallus, slips on a banana skin, struggles back to his feet, slips again, then introduces himself to the crowd as Boogalloo before launching into what he hopes will boost, yet further, his chances of the top job. Only it doesn't work out quite that way, particularly as potential supporters are already tittering at the speaking phallus called Boogalloo skidding about on banana skins and assuming this is some kind of a comedy break from the songs they've been singing along to. The titters become chuckles then guffaws, however, as instead of saying the intended "Fight with me in the upcoming general election in which our zone has many electoral votes, brother goblins—and victorious we shall be," as the phallus turns into Gobshyte, he says, "Fart with me in the uppity crumbling general erection in twitch our zoo has lotta electrical volts, bogling bladders—and wickyprurious we shall pee." That's the revised version. The actual one is interspersed every other word with the rhythmically emphatic "blurg-buh-*tom*," at the insertion of every one of which Gobshyte turns to show his naked bottom and slap himself on it. The single sentence takes upwards of ten minutes to deliver by which time the audience, egged on by Gabi, James, and Norbert, has first become hysterical and then, as humour morphs into anger, begun to chuck rotten gryphon's eggs and simurgh turds, obliging Gobshyte to slip so badly on another banana skin he falls off the stage flat on his face and deflates like a punctured balloon, making farting noises as he does so, at which, the crowd breaks in thunderous clapping. Or, as a bemused and cerebrally dysfunctional Gobshyte hears it: "The cloud crapped."

~ * ~

In the second dream, much the same happens to Gobollox, with a few variations, of course. Same general message but with a different setting, different cast of characters, and in Gobollox's case, a different screwed up message to stutter. Also, in KayCee's dream, he initially appears not as a phallus but a vagina on stilts, which is pretty far-fetched, but you know how it is with dreams. When KayCee recounted them to Brosista, Gabi, James and Norbert at a planning meeting the following morning, they all had a good laugh, although it was only Gabi who understood their provenance.

"All we need now is to translate your sleeping imagination into reality." She chuckled as the puzzled others asked for an explanation.

"It was all your idea, girlfriend, *you* tell them," said KayCee.

So Gabi did and they loved it.

"And you really think you could re-programme Gobshyte to behave that way?" said Brosista.

KayCee shrugged modestly. "If I could turn a ruby into a man-eating python and lioness, it shouldn't be too hard. You know as well as I do, Brosy, what sorts of tricks we elves have up our sleeves."

"Indeed, my dear. It's just mine have become a little rusty through disuse."

"Well, we'll see what we can do to bring them back to life. How about you and I pool our resources and work together on this?"

"Raaf, raaf!" said Cyndy, which was unusual for an Italian Greyhound, a breed normally reticent when it comes to barking. But this was a special occasion.

"Ookay then. It should be fun," said Brosista, stroking the tiny dog's boney head.

"And Gabi also reckoned you could tamper with the guy's toot machine," said Norbert. "How would that work?"

"By hacking into it with a new set of codes. Easy peasy," said KayCee. "And you will remember the mayhem caused in the human zone through Internet messaging. Presidents elected who never should have been, fake news spread to the masses, all of that. It's how populism blossomed, am I right?"

"Spot on," said James, who was still fretting over Facebook and Cambridge Analytica. "But Gabi, Norbert, and I will still get to travel around doing our comedy routines?" he added, having already practised the Laurel and Hardy bowler hat trick with Norbert.

"Of course, you shall. It will take Brosista and me a wee while to test drive our re-programming. Trial runs and all that sort of thing to be sure everything is working whenever we want it. Meanwhile, Fairyland is yours. Think of yourselves as the warm-up act."

Gabi, James, and Norbert grinned. They were starting to enjoy the ride. How long they had been away from St Ives they didn't know and didn't care. This was more fun than they'd had in their whole lives so far.

~ * ~

While KayCee and Brosista tinkered with magical manipulations, their human guests prepared for their peregrinations around Fairyland by practising jokes and slapstick routines. The trip was to be under the guidance of a specially appointed elf guide called Plunkett, who had been apprised of the importance of his/her mission in a top-level meeting with Brosista.

"This is a great honour for you, Plunky," s/he had explained, " and one which I hope will beneficially affect all of Fairyland's tomorrows."

"Wow," replied Plunkett, who was even smaller than the average elf but made up for it with an intelligence quotient greater than the sum of four other elves twice his/her size. Down the yesterdays, s/he had become a constant aide-de-camp to Brosista, with whom many secrets were shared. And so it was on this occasion as s/he became party to the plan Gabi and KayCee had concocted and the role the humans were to play in it.

"Wow," Plunkett repeated.

"Yes, pretty important for us all, as you will doubtless understand. And they're decent types who have offered their services in the resolution of our little difficulties so you can be sure to trust them," Brosista explained. "A lot smaller than they would be back where they come from, of course, so they would fit in here. But they're reasonably pretty nonetheless."

"Like little mini-humans."

"Indeed."

"And will I understand their language? Both you and KayCee have been to the human zone and can say things in er...um..."

"English."

"*Ing*litch, that's the fellow. But I have never made that trip, and there's no time for me to learn the lingo in only a couple of tomorrows, is there?"

"Don't worry, Plunky, KayCee will provide you with a special pill which will allow it to enter your brain overnight. And if it is only marginally successful, which I doubt, as a reserve resource you will carry with you at all times a tiny gizmo around your neck which will take over in case all else fails."

"Wow," Plunkett re-repeated. "Hi-tech, eh?"

"The highest."

"And I shall take them where?"

"Wherever they want to go, although I shall provide an itinerary I'll suggest you follow. They have already visited some of our friendly neighbours, so no point in meeting them again. Where their impact will be greatest is in zones over which Gobshyte holds some sway. *These* are the places most in need of a little softening up, one feels."

"With dancing and laughing and funny japes."

"Quite so. I'm sure they will show you a few of those before you depart."

"I look forward to it. I like laughing."

"Don't we all? And it is high time our good folk returned to the practice instead of hurling insults at each other."

"And at you."

Unaccustomed as s/he was to self-concern, Brosista smiled wanly and nodded. "Yes, it would be nice if that were to cease, too."

"I shall do my utmost to ensure it, dear friend."

"Thank you, Plunky. Thank you, indeed. No better comrade could a person wish for. And now, perhaps, you would care to meet our human friends?"

"With great pleasure."

And so, it was that Brosista led Plunkett across to the barn where Norbert, James, and Gabi were busy trying to adapt some human comedy moments to what they hoped would amuse fairies. It was all a bit shot-in-the-darkish, but included a lot of slipping over, particularly on banana skins in preparation for Gobshyte's mishaps, although it also featuring plenty of tripping over tree roots, falling into ponds, being pooed on by gryphons, unexplained yet embarrassing farting noises—and, of course, pie throwing, all of which Norbert excelled at, given these were the mainstays of German humour. James had also proposed a John Cleese's Ministry of Funny Walks routine refined to reflect the militaristic gaits of both Gobshyhte (James) and Gobollox (Norbert) who, of course, bang into each other while trying to look soldierly and fall over. In her condition, Gabi had been told under *no* circumstances to fall over and had opted instead for a pierrot face exhibiting inappropriate responses to everyday situations—nose wrinkling and disgusted looks when flattered, schadenfreude tut-tutting and gesticulations at the misfortunes of her colleagues, that sort of thing. Plus, she was planning make-up to give her the classic white clown's face, both sad and mad. In all of this, there was naturally no linguistic content, which James claimed was a pity because he had collected a lot of particularly graphic limericks down the years. He was in the middle of the one beginning, "There was a young man from Devises" (the last line is "the other was big and won prizes") when Brosista knocked on the door and asked if s/he might introduce the guide for their travels around the land.

"Pleasetameetcha, guys, I'm Plunkett but you can call me Plunky," said Plunkett, seeing as the language pill s/he'd been given spoke

American. "I'm your guide and interpreter for the travels. Gonna be a lotta fun, I can see that already."

"Plunky is my oldest and wisest friend and counselor. S/he knows Fairyland backwards and forwards and inside out," said Brosista, as Gabi, James, and Norbert introduced themselves in turn, then took the tiny elf by the hand and shook it.

"Great to have you on board," said Norbert. "We'd have been pretty damn hopeless wandering around by ourselves."

"A pleasure," said Plunkett. "Brosy has filled me in on all the background, and I am, like, A-1 in favour of the plan. Gonna be a gas."

"A gas and one hopes a success," said James. "You think the idea has wings?"

"Sure I do. 'A day without laughter is a day wasted,' right?" said Plunkett, whose neck gizmo had also provided him with a few quotes it thought might be useful. This one came from Charlie Chaplin.

"Although it's not simple laughter we're peddling," said Gabi. "You might even think of it as the devil's, if you knew its purpose."

Plunkett nodded and smiled. "I do know its purpose and concur fully with it, Miss Human. After all, humour has many faces and can do all kindsa tricks. We ain't just hyenas, am I right?"

"Spot on," said James. "As we know from Milan Kindera's *The Book of Laughter and Forgetting.*"

Norbert nodded, frowned, and muttered, "Nineteen sixty-eight after the Prague spring, right? When the Soviet tanks came rolling into town? But still those old Czechs kept laughing. You know what they daubed in red paint on walls all around town?"

James shook his head. He'd read the book and liked it, but had no personal experience of the country.

"Czechs four, Soviets two. That was the result of a recent ice hockey game."

"Wow," said Plunkett who had no idea who or what Czechs, Soviets or ice hockey were but got the general idea especially after Gabi, with poignant memories of the old East Berlin, explained the potential of such an action.

Brosista was impressed. "Which in a way is exactly what we're asking of you folk over here in Fairyland."

"To laugh the bad guys outta Dodge," said Plunkett, spoken by Neck Gizmo. Plunkett had no more idea of Dodge City than he did of Soviets or Czechs but, hey, it was one helluva plan.

"Precisely," said Norbert. "And, whether you know it or not, we Berliners owe a debt of gratitude to your KayCee for sorting out our little problem with nasties. Not with laughter, but even so."

Plunkett wanted to hear more about that, but Brosista cut in saying, "Look, it's getting late and, if you'll excuse me, I need to get back to KayCee who's still working away on our Gobshyte programming. Why don't I leave you here with your new friends, Plunky? I'm sure you and they will have many more interesting stories to exchange."

"Fine with us," said Norbert.

"Fine with us, too," chorused the baby gryphons, hippogriffs, simurghs, a chimera, three cats, a chameleon, a toad, a pig, and seventeen rabbits in a variety of welcoming croaks, shrieks, miaows, grunts and some other unworldly noises.

Plunkett laughed. "Thanks, you animal guys. I'd almost forgotten about you."

Twenty-seven

And so it was, that leaving Brosista and KayCee to put the finishing touches to their Gobshyte mind games, Plunkett and his humies—that's what Plunkett called humans—set off on their softening-up tour of Fairyland...Norbert, Gabi, and James all having agreed to the itinerary Brosista had prescribed.

"No point in preaching to the converted," Norbert said as Plunkett teleported them far away from Brosista's tranquil zone to the grisly areas in which dwelt mainly the goblins and boggarts.

"Better gird your loins though, guys," Plunkett warned, "these are tough places so don't expect an easy ride."

"All full of hillbillies and rednecks," Neck Gizmo added, believing the humies would need a bit of context from their own zone.

"Your lips never moved when you said that, Plunky," said Gabi. "Are you a ventriloquist as well as a guide?"

Plunkett arched an eyebrow and shrugged. "You had to find out sometime. Like I got this little dealie around my neck that knows stuff?" he said, opening his blouse to reveal Neck Gizmo, who winked an electronic eye, and said, "Hi, guys. Nice knowin' y'all. You can call me Neckie."

Gabi and company laughed, and said, "Hi right back to you, Neckie."

They stopped laughing, however, when they discovered whither they'd been teleported. Peering about, there were no more of the grassy glades, farmland, and little lakes of Brosista's zone in evidence, just scrubby undergrowth, dirt tracks, and what looked like a dying forest. So this was where Gobshyte's acolytes hung out. Hillbillies and rednecks were apt comparators from the US states whence Dougal Klank had garnered so much of his support. Judging by the territory, Plunkett was right, this job wasn't going to be a piece of cake, not at all it wasn't.

It was Gabi who spotted the first pair of red eyes glaring at them from behind a stunted tree. "Shuh-shuh-*shit*," she said, jumping backwards into James's arms. "Luh-luh-look over *there*. A wuh-wuh-*wolf*."

Plunkett held up a calming palm. "That's no wolf, lady, that's an angry goblin. Just remember our plan, guys. Show no fear, okay? *No* fear. That'll only let 'em win before we've even gotten started. What you gotta do is take it on the chin, roll with the blows, an' come back laughing. You all got that?" he was saying as the goblin, accompanied by two pals with long tangled beards down to their knees, sprang out from behind the tree and took to sticking out their stained tongues, spitting on the scrubby ground, and snarling foul Gobshyte-esque oaths.

"Grrrr, grrr, fuck off back where you came from, fuckin' foreigners," they growled in Goblinish, thumbing their noses and finger-slitting their throats.

After all his years as a Stasi soldier and mobster, Norbert was the one best placed to follow Plunkett's counsel. Legion were the foes he'd had to face down in his time. Okay, back then he'd mainly just shot them and walked away, and now, he was required to do the precise opposite, but he rose to the occasion. As James, Gabi, and Plunkett watched on, he merely walked over towards the pugnacious goblins, twice faux tripping and sprawling on the ground before each time climbing back to his feet, dusting himself down, chuckling at his own clumsiness, and when he finally reached them, tickling each one and himself with a special tickling stick before bursting out into guffaws.

Which, as you can imagine, surprised the goblins—and the boggart who'd joined them. This wasn't the response they'd been expecting, nothing like it. Anger at the very least was their assumption. At which they would have stood their ground and given these humies—as their leader Grymph had suddenly recognised these creatures—six kinds of shit. But laughter not *at* them but *with* them was nowhere on the agenda, although...although...it did chime with a distant arcane memory buried in some yesterday or another. Of camp fires, and dancing, and singing, and jokes, and...

"Ugh?" said Grymph, unable to stop giggling girlishly at the tickling stick treatment Norbert was administering to him. Lying flat on his back with both legs and one arm waggling in the air.

"Plunky," said James. "Would now be a good time for us to join the party and for you to do a little interpreting?"

"The best, dude," said Plunky via his language pill.

"You do *speak* Goblinish?"

"Like a native," said Plunky, before reeling off a string of consonants apparently unconnected by any vowels. "Follow me."

~ * ~

Thereafter things went pretty smoothly. Having explained to the goblins, s/he and the humies meant them no harm; they were just doing a little showbiz-type tour of Fairyland to try out some new comedy material; that was all, Grymph and company stopped growling oaths and spitting feathers and merely stood about looking quizzical. It was Groyne, a relatively junior goblin, who finally emerged from the huddle and asked Plunkett quite politely if he and his friends might witness a few examples of the humies' comedy show.

"You up for that, guys?" Plunkett asked James, Norbert, and Gabi who, pleased at the goblins' new acquiescence, nodded their agreement. "Just, ya know, a bit of pie throwing, mebbe a cartwheel or two, couple of funny walks?"

"No problemo," said Norbert.

"Tell you what," James suggested. "Why don't we run a *pie-*throwing contest?"

"Which we will lose, right?" said Gabi. "We throw all our pies, but miss and fall over and…"

"Then they throw their pies like we were Aunt Sallies, and every one is a winner," Norbert completed the sentence for her.

"And every time you get hit, you wipe the cream off your faces, do dumb grins and laugh like hell," said Plunkett. "Only you don't *all* get it, only the boys. You, Mistress Gabi, can do your clown act and skulk around pointing at them like they were the stupidest dorks you ever saw in your whole life. Wanna give that a whirl?"

"Great idea," said Gabi, "only I want to join in, too…it'll do the baby no harm. I can dress as a clown, but I'm still going to take the pies."

"Ookey dokey," said Neck Gizmo. "That cool with you other guys?"

"No problemo at all," said Norbert. "Away you go and explain the rules of the game to our new friends while we get the pies ready. Equal numbers on each team, right? Three of them, three of us. And we stand five paces apart."

"You got it, bro," said Plunkett, taking Groyne by his grimy mitt and sauntering over to apprise his pals of James's suggestion.

At first they frowned at Plunkett and exchanged puzzled looks.

"*Pie* throwing?" said Blonk the boggart in ropey Goblinish. "What kind of nonsense is *that*?"

"Just a bit of fun, that's all."

"And the winners get prizes?" Grymph wanted to know.

"Each one on the team gets a little gold cup," Plunkett assured him. "Plus, of course, the satisfaction of being the winners."

This further confused the goblin gang who stepped away a couple of paces to discuss the pros and cons of such a game. If they won, that would be fine. But then the humies would be angry, wouldn't they? And what if they had weapons? Rumour had it humies carried little banging iron things that shot more pieces of iron. And if the humies won, that would be humiliating for the goblins, so…

Overhearing, Plunkett calmed such concerns in a couple of all-consonantal Goblinish sentences, assuring the group these humies *didn't* carry guns, that's what the iron things were called, and should they lose would be good sports about it, promise.

"Good *sports*?" Groyne asked, there being no such concept in the modern day Gobshyte-run goblin zone.

Tired of all this explaining, Plunkett said, "Listen guys, just pick a team of three, okay. It's gonna be *fun*."

"Honest Injun," said Neck Gizmo in Goblinish. Pointlessly, seeing as no-one including Plunkett knew what injuns were, let alone if they were honest.

Anyway, *any*way, eventually the goblins picked their team (Grymph, Groyne and Blonk) to face Norbert, James and Gabi, and the event got under way after the toss of a specially carved flat stone with a head on one side and a tail on the other to see who went first. Plunkett officiated as both captains (Grymph and Norbert) stepped forward, but there was an inevitable delay when Norbert stuck out a hand for the traditional shake and Grymph dived to the ground covering his head and whimpering.

"Oh, for Oberon's *sakes*," said Plunkett. "He's not gonna *hit* you."

And so it went, delay after delay of one kind or another until finally Norbert won the toss and the game got going. James's pie stuck to his hand and, in trying to undo it, he smeared it in his own face, burst out laughing, fell to the floor and was disqualified by Plunkett.

The goblins chuckled, sensing their advantage.

Norbert's pie flew high and wide, ending up in the stunted branches of a tree whence it leaked gunge onto the ground. "*Scheiße*," he said. Also pointlessly, because not even Plunkett knew what that meant. But Norbert too was chuckling self-deprecatingly, so that was okay.

More goblin chuckling, then it was Gabi's turn. Looking athletic and practised at the event, she took the pie masterfully in her right hand then inexplicably tripped and tossed it in the air. Which might not have been so bad had its fall back to earth not been broken by her face, causing it to crease in helpless mirth.

Goblins guffawing fit to bust.

Then, as team humie got back in a line, it was team goblins/ boggart's turn. And you know what happened, don't you? A bull's eye every time for Grymph, Groyne and Blonk until Plunkett announced the final score of Humies 0, Goblins/Boggart 3.

It was as Grymph, Groyne and Blonk were prancing about being congratulated by each other and the audience of their fellow goblins that the strangest thing of all happened to them. In the midst of the presentation of gold cups, James, Norbert and Gabi—all covered in pie fillings—marched over and sportingly shook each one by the hand.

The goblins didn't know what to make of it, but it seemed genuine enough, so...

So peace broke out, that was what, and once the hand-shaking was over, the goblins invited Plunkett and his humies hack to their hovels in the middle of the dying forest where they spent the evening carousing, dancing, and listening to each other's songs. Translated for them by Plunkett, the humie ditty they liked the best was John Lennon's "Imagine," especially the line about all the people sharing all the world. Hard to believe after the animus of recent times but, as noted, fairies, including goblins and boggarts, have *very* short memories and by midnight, it was only the fun they'd had in the course of this one day they remembered. And who had been the providers of it? *Humies*, that was who. And, of course, Plunkett the elf from the Brosista zone. So much for foreigners being the bad guys Gobshyte said they were. By bedtime, Norbert, James and Gabi had been introduced all around the village with invitations to come back whenever they wanted.

Plunkett was delighted. "Well done, guys," he said as the quartet lay down to sleep in a specially cleared but, nonetheless, still thorny bed of what might once have been roses. "Let's hope the same trick works in all our travels."

Both a little squiffy after all their cups of dandelion whisky, Norbert and James merely gurgled assent, but pregnant teetotaller Gabi was even more optimistic than Plunkett.

"No need for only hope," she said. "I know in my bones it will."

"And if it don't you'll eat your hat?" said Neck Gizmo.

"Neckie, if it doesn't, I'll eat *two* hats."

Having no idea what hat-eating referred to, Plunkett nonetheless grinned and, through his language pill, said, "Atta-girl," before rolling over and starting to snore.

And you know what, folks? Gabi's conviction of success was richly rewarded, so no need for eating any form of clothing. The pie throwing template remained in place for all their coming visits—although with minor variations to include greater emphasis on Gabi's pierrot role—then there the funny walks and clowning, but the results, including the notion of sharing their worlds, were always the same. By the time KayCee and Brosista had completed their work on Gobshyte's language and general demeanour, the next occasion on which the wannabe leader of Fairyland pranced behind a podium with populism on his mind, the stage was set for a very different reception.

Twenty-eight

Gobshyte didn't get it. What the hell was happening to him? Alone, or with Gobollox in his luxury cave, everything went just fine. Up and down in front of his mirror he strode, honing his orations to the point of what he considered perfection, jabbing his fingers about theatrically, and glaring meaningfully with not the hint of a mistake. No need for notes to remind him, no future role for Gobollox to sit in the front row of the audience with cue signs, the performance was just about as smooth and impressive as it possibly could be.

But on the sole occasion he had recently ventured onto a local stage for a spot of electioneering, weird things started happening—tripping over banana skins that should never have been there, opening his mouth only for a great jumble of flapdoodle to come dribbling out, calling himself Boogaloo and, worst of all, finding himself dressed as a penis. No, actually that *wasn't* the very worst thing of all. What was even more humiliating was the reception he got from the crowd—hoots of laughter, erstwhile solid supporters tearing up their GOBSHYTE FOREVER banners and hurling the fragments at him. At *him* of all goblins, their leader-in-waiting. It was as if someone had wound them up before they even came. Like it was some audience participation slapstick comedy show they'd got tickets for.

"What...the...fuck...is...goin'...*on*?" he asked Gobollox back in the cave on the night after this fiasco.

"Dunno, do I boss? Only I didn't wanna tell you before, but the same thing's happened to me. Last time I was out bendin' minds, I kept fallin' over and talkin' bollocks too...only I was dressed as a fanny on big thin legs"

"Stilts," Gobshyte corrected.

"Call 'em what you like, boss. It was the 'fanny' I didn't like. 'Specially when the whole crowd started chantin' it and throwin' stuff at me."

"What stuff?"

"Poo an' explodin' bags of piss."

Gobshyte stared off and shook his head. "No good askin' *you* what the fuck's goin' on then."

"Not a lot of good, boss. What're we gonna *do*? Things go on like this, we ain't got no chance of topplin' the Brosista bitchman, have we?"

Gobshyte re-shook his head, this time mournfully. "Bollocks," he said.

"Yes boss?" said Gobollox, mishearing his name.

"Not you, *life*. The slings and arrows of outrageous bollocks."

"Tell you what though, boss."

"What? And it better be good."

"It's a cunnin' ruse I just thought up," said Gobollox. "How about if you and me do a show to*gether*, narmean? Then if there's any trouble we can look out for each other, can't we? You slip, I pick you up. *I* slip, you pick *me* up. *You* start talking giggleyshit, *I* get you back on track. Like bruvvers, we help each other out. Show solidarity folk should learn from."

Gobshyte mused on this for a bit. "Okay," he then said. "Only what if I'm dressed as a dick and you a fanny?"

"You'll just have to flirt wiv me, won'tcha boss? Make you look pretty sexy that would."

"There is that to it," Gobshyte admitted. Virility was one of his key selling points, or so he reckoned.

"So d'you wanna give my cunnin' ruse a go or dontcha?"

"We'll give it a trial run," Gobshyte replied grudgingly.

Back in Brosista's hut, s/he and KayCee smiled as they watched this scene from the Gobshyte cave, thanks to a secretly installed TV transmitter.

"I just love it when a plan comes together," said KayCee.

~ * ~

The little details of what happened at Gobshyte's and Gobollox's next (and final) gig shall be left to your imaginations. Suffice it to say, however, that Gobollox's cunning ruse didn't work. In fact, it was a turkey of such gargantuan proportions as to render Gobshyte's aspirations to the top job dead in the water. How fervently he had *hoped* the recent past would be forgotten—which was a reasonable calculation given fairies' short memory spans—and this would be the very performance that would conclusively seal his claim to glory! But that's hubris for you. And, to be fair, how could he have known of the special GRHRP (Gobshyte Revulsion and Hilarity Recall Powder) KayCee had asked Plunkett to sprinkle in the drinking water at each of the humie troupe's comedic shows? No way, that was how.

"Dirty tricks," I hear you say, and you may have a point. But what's a little memory enhancement by comparison with the sorts of below the belt chicanery Gobshyte had been up to for many, many yesterdays? Anyway, the point shall remain moot. The fact of the matter, as evinced at Gobshyte's and Gobollox's last desperate attempt at popularity, was that no fairy—even ones as fickle as fairies can oftentimes be—was going to put their cross against a candidate who was not only unable to stand, didn't know his own name and spoke in riddles but, as a finale, tried to make love to his own second-in-command. So it was that Gobshyte and Gobollox were consigned to a zone of forgetfulness, unusual even by Fairyland standards.

Brosista was over the moon at the outcome and translated her over-the-moonness into concrete action by elevating KayCee to the role of Vice Leader of the fairy world, Plunkett to Minister of Inter-Humie Affairs, and bestowed on Gabi, James and Norbert the honorary title of FOAFF (Friend of All Fairy Folk), granting them and their closest family the freedom of Fairyland for the foreseeable future—i.e. tomorrow. But now, knowing what 'tomorrow' meant in fairy terms, the humies were delighted. How great it would be for Ernest, Georgina, Stephanie and William—never mind whatever baby Cockburn Gabi eventually produced—to have such a prospect available to them. Deep into the night of Brosista's re-election the celebrations continued. It was almost as though sanity had returned after a crazy night of disturbed dreams.

In the speech celebrating her re-election to the leadership, Brosista characteristically underplayed her own role in recent events, citing instead those she had honoured as the ones primarily responsible for her success, particularly the humans.

"My friends," s/he concluded, "the most important thing for you now always to try to remember…"

Self-mocking laughter from the assembled hordes of fairies of all stripes.

"…is never ever again to allow fear of the other to be hijacked by those who would avail themselves of such distrust with evil intentions. That way condemnation lies, where there should be understanding, suspicion where there should be cooperation, hatred where there should be love. Together we have hope; divided we fall into despair. On this auspicious occasion, I beseech you to remain true to the fairy traditions we so cherish. Search your memories for it…

More self-mockery from the hordes, but some clapping, too.

"…and always use your ears so you can hear and keep your eyes open so you can see. For this will bring life to thee."

~ * ~

These were the words James heard himself mumbling as, stretched out on his bench in Queen Mary's Gardens, he opened eyes and peered about in the gathering dusk.

"Ugh? What the…?" he said, looking at his watch and finding it was two hours and forty-six minutes since he'd last checked it.

"You've been asleep, mate," was the answer he received from gardener Harry George, who was leaning on his rake behind the bench. "Dreamin' by the look of the twitching you were doin'. So I left you alone, didn't I? No good disturbin' a bloke when he's dreamin' is what my ole dad used to say an' I reckon he was right. Just hope you enjoyed it, that's all. Only you'd better get goin' now. We're shuttin' up shop soon."

Twisting around, James stared. "Dreaming?"

"Yeah. Not just twitchin' but making little baby-like gurgly noises some of the time an' big gasps at other times. Bleedin' excitin' dream it must've been."

"Bloody hell," said James, raising himself on an elbow.

"Anyhow, like I said, it's home time now, chummy. Gotta make sure we don't leave nobody here overnight, right? Some say there's ghosties around 'ere when the darkness comes."

"Okay, but could you just give me ten minutes?" said James, fumbling in his bag for the Moleskine notebook he carried with him at all times to jot down his latest ideas for stories. Other, younger writers carried iPads and mini-voice recorders for such insights, but not James. Still a pen and paper man was he.

"Ten minutes then I'll be back to fetch you."

"Okay," said James, delving into an already poor memory for any fragment of the dream he at least remembered he'd *had*. And a pretty climactic note it had ended on, he reckoned.

But you know how it is with dreams. We've been through that (see above somewhere). How, if they return at all, they come in ill-assorted, ill-connected fragments, leaving only faint and normally inconclusive sensations—of sex or James Bondish adventures if you're lucky, but more often of irreparable failure, angst, and impending doom. And so it was for James. Bits of the former, plenty of the latter, even fairies involved, for God's sake. On the other hand, on...the...other...hand, hang on a minute, had he not somehow been partly responsible for saving not only *this* world but the fairies' one, too? James reckoned so. It hadn't been just him, though. There was also some bisexual elf involved. What was its name again? Macy? Spacey? Tracy? Some name like that. In dribs and drabs, the images were starting to come back to him.

It was as he was jabbing at his notebook, his imagination running wild when for so many months it had been so blocked he thought he'd never write a book again, that there came a voice to his right.

"Nice. A Golden Celebration I think," it said in a faint German accent.

"Ugh?" said James, turning to see a tall blonde with the finest bottom he'd ever witnessed in Queen Mary's Gardens.

"The rose, a Golden Celebration?"

"Jubilee. *Diamond* Jubilee."

"*Ach so.* May I sit with you?"

"I don't know. I'm busy. The gardens are closing soon and..."

"So let us leave together. I have a car waiting. I am Gabi, by the way. And you are?"

"James. James Cockburn."

"The *writer*?"

Flattered in the way of any failed writer when recognized and attracted by Gabi's hair, bottom, and general Germanity, James succumbed to her invitation without demur.

"Maybe this, finally, is my lucky day," he thought, ambling along beside her in what he thought of as a sultry manner. "First the dream of my new book, now my dream woman. Helloo the good times."

"King's Cross, please," Gabi told the cabbie before they headed off down Chester Road to the Outer Circle of Regent's Park.

THE END
or
THE BEGINNING

Meet Paddy Bostock

Paddy Bostock was born in Liverpool and holds a B.A. in Modern Languages and History, a PGDip TESL, and a PhD in English Literature. Down the years he has been a barman, a road worker, a songwriter, an educational researcher, a translator, a book reviewer, a university lecturer and Chair of Department, and a high school mentor. He lives in London with his wife, writer Dani Cavallaro, and likes animals and bicycles.

Other Works From The Pen Of
Paddy Bostock

Mole Smith and the Diamond Studded Pistol - Mole Smith needs to solve an ancient mystery.

Two Down - Worry about your cellphone! Others may have spooky designs on it.

La Joie de Vivre - "Cherchez la femme!" — words Ambler will come to wish he'd never heard...

For the Love of a Woman — Family: you can't live with them; you can't live without them...

Foot Soldiers - When will we ever learn...?

Hand in Glove - Never judge a zebra by its stripes...

Noddy in Wonderland - Will wonders never cease?

Peace on Earth - Peace on earth? Don't bet on it...

The Basque Head Case - Of heads found...and lost!

The Bore - Funny thing, boredom...

The Hanging — Nothing is set in stone.

Chosen — It's only rock 'n roll, but...

Letter to Our Readers

Enjoy this book?

You can make a difference

As an independent publisher, Wings ePress, Inc. does not have the financial clout of the large New York Publishers. We can't afford large magazine spreads or subway posters to tell people about our quality books.

But, we do have something much more effective and powerful than ads. We have a large base of loyal readers.

Honest Reviews help bring the attention of new readers to our books.

If you enjoyed this book, we would appreciate it if you would spend a few minutes posting a review on the site where you purchased this book or on the Wings ePress, Inc. webpages at: https://wingsepress.com/

9 781613 096093